DARK
CLOUDS
BRING
WATERS

DARK CLOUDS BRING WATERS

I.R. RIDLEY

www.v-books.co.uk

Twitter: @VBooks10
Facebook: vbooks10
Instagram: vbookspublishing

Cover design by Steve Leard
Typeset by seagulls.net

ISBN: 978-1-7396396-2-4

Where there is sorrow,
there is holy ground

Oscar Wilde

Tuesday, 11 May 1993

Dear Billie,

I'm sorry it's come to this after ten years. I once loved you deeply but now that love has been overshadowed by what's happened and all that we've become, sad to say. I just couldn't go on like that nor live under the same roof as you any longer. Drama, sound and fury have become too tiresome and overwhelming for this ageing stick-in-the-mud, as you described him.

The envelope will show our New Forest postmark but it will be for the last time. I'm writing this the day before I leave. It's because I can no longer stomach conflict after that final straw and didn't want you coming down here creating more mayhem. So, by the time this letter has reached you, I'll have left this address. I'm going away with Christine and we intend to make a new life together. I've resigned from the University, as has Christine, and we've found new jobs abroad. Fortunately, they understood our need to get away after that shocking episode.

I'm sure you will say that it was Christine who split us up. But she was a natural conclusion to the sickness and sadness of our relationship, Billie, and not the cause of its ending. Truth is, the differences in us that seemed to attract and complement each other for so long just became a gulf between us. Ambition always drove you, while the quiet, academic life sufficed for me. The age gap between us, which seemed to intrigue you when you first came to Birmingham, only highlighted in the last couple of years that we were no longer compatible.

I know I frustrated you. That was obvious in the bouts of your temper that frightened me. You regularly telling me that I was boring. I became confused when sometimes you wanted sex regularly then would go months without speaking of it. Until it stopped altogether. I did think that during those times you were sleeping with another man occasionally, as I believe you did in our university summer vacations apart.

It doesn't matter any more, Billie. It's not worth picking at the scabs further. All is said and done after that row to end all rows. Or at least I hope it is. The New Forest house will have to be sold and the profits divided equally since we both put in the same amount. Given your stated desire to move to London permanently in search of more stimulating work and a new start, it seems the best solution. I hope now that I have left, it will speed the process along and you won't keep blocking things by insisting the house is worth more than it is.

It's a shame that our ending has been so rushed and acrimonious but that is unfortunately how it has worked out. I've appointed a solicitor in Southampton and he'll be in touch soon. I'm willing to share my permanent address overseas at some point but I need to be sure from him that the dust has settled and that I – and Christine – are not going to be subjected to any more frightening scenes. I really want us to be more civilised towards each other so that we can be adult about all this and settle financially, and into new lives. I wish you well with yours and wherever it leads you next.

Slán,
Adam.

1

Once Luke would have been annoyed that the driver was not there waiting, all the more so as the heat in here was stifling. Back in the day, she'd always booked the car and the sign that the chauffeur used to hold up would say "Miss Billie". He smiled ruefully now at the irony of those two words, those double-meaning words, as he contemplated the flurry of motion that was the same at airport arrival halls the world over. Amid the blend of those pacing listlessly in wait and others just in and keen to be on their way, footsteps light with anticipation, he stood alone and motionless. It was as if he was in one of those movie shots where a character is rigid, with just the camera – in his case now, his eyes – panning the scene. In fact, he'd felt like that a lot these past two years, ten months, one week and four days; not just that life was going on around his isolated self but also that there was simply nothing worth experiencing the anxiety of agitation for any more. Even if he did hope that this trip – the first he had felt able to make since the pandemic and since... well, *since* – might bring something different.

Flying, or more accurately crashing, no longer bothered him; the worst that could have happened in his life had already happened. But all had gone well enough with the flight. There had been no delays and in fact he was into Cristoforo Colombo ten minutes ahead of schedule. It was one reason why he and Billie had come here each year. The airport was small, with comparatively few flights, and was easy to get in and out of despite its cramped facilities. They could be on the roads above Genoa within fifteen minutes of landing and at their favourite hotel within another thirty.

He gazed around now and waited five minutes or so but, once he was sure that there was no figure holding up a rectangular whiteboard bearing his felt-tipped name, he eased his way through the loitering relatives and drivers out to the drop-off area. He remembered being in this spot heading home from their first holiday here. She had pointed out a yellow sign with a black motif of a plane pointing skywards on it and the words "Kiss and Fly" underneath, which almost seemed to define her, embrace her passion, especially her passion for travel. 'So Italian,' she'd said, smiling. She always noticed these things. He'd been in a rush back then, in his stressed state of trying to avoid stress, to get to the check-in queue ahead of others, and failed to take in such a joyous incidental himself. But she was so in her element, of the moment, aware, alive. Yes, alive. These days, to spoil the memory, it added: "(Maximum 12 minutes)". Once, he would have found something witty and/or fruity to say for her about the new restriction, maybe something about how twelve minutes of kissing and flying would be a marathon session for him these days. But now, funny still felt beyond him. Something of a drawback for someone who'd made his living writing comedy.

It was in the June, some nine months after the diagnosis, three since the chemotherapy had ended. Her hair was still growing back, in patches, thicker and clumpier than it had been. She was wearing that green shift dress, cream jacket and matching ballet pumps, and sporting her big brown Jackie O tortoiseshell sunglasses. The treatment had stolen some of her life but none of her life force. She'd beamed on seeing the sign and now a smile came naturally, almost involuntarily, to his lips. Whenever she'd travelled anywhere after that, she would text him from her seat on the plane just ahead of take-off: "X fly."

It had been hot then but now it was steaming, unseasonably so for early autumn. He had chosen this weekend in mid-September because he had expected the weather to have cooled – and because of the absence of schoolchildren, quieter roads and hotel – but it must be, what, at least 30 degrees this early afternoon? He fanned his face with his panama, feeling a bead of sweat drip from his temple. The sensory assault of Mediterranean heat brought back another memory of Billie, at another airport, from a quarter of a century ago.

His divorce had not long come through and she'd come for a few days to the villa he'd rented in the hills overlooking Nice to meet Jude, then four, on father and son's summer holiday together. It hadn't gone especially well. Though Jude would warm to her as the years wore on, at that age, with his parents having split up a year earlier, he was an angry young soul and Billie just wasn't his mother. He could not be expected then to realise that it was not she who had taken their father away from him and his mum. Indeed, he couldn't be expected to see that it was his mother who had made the decision after meeting the man who was now Jude's stepfather, and at that time he did not need his world shattered further by such a thing as truth.

Billie had been nervous, naturally, but had done her best to blend in with them rather than impose herself on their relationship. A friend of Jude's choosing and a nanny for the week also helped. Here, now, the heat triggered the memory of standing in her embrace at Nice airport as she prepared to depart and him being keen for it to be over so that he could get back to Jude, even if the boy was occupied with his friend and safe enough with the nanny. He worried too much back then, about not being with his son for an afternoon, yes, but also that Jude might tell his mother that Daddy had left him for some hours. The habit of doing anything to evade her cold ire died hard.

'All right,' Billie had snapped. 'I'll be gone soon enough.'

'No, I...' he'd started to protest, but her instinct about his impatience was right. She always did have smart instincts. He'd been torn between her, the new love of his life, and his son, his eternal love.

Odd, he thought now, the shifting significances of memory and memories. He'd smiled at the sign, recalling a warm, reassuring moment, but very quickly further contemplation revealed an unnerving intrusion of tensions from long ago, from a time when each other's quirks and foibles were emerging to dilute the potency of new attraction. Memories could soothe and sustain him in his emptiness, and could shine a spotlight on the enormity of what had been lost. They could also bring a regret at the way he had behaved and handled matters on occasions that still returned to taunt him, a regret that grew with depth of thought.

'Signor Jessop?' came a voice behind him. 'Signor Luke Jessop?'

He turned abruptly and saw a squat man in grey trousers and an open-necked, short-sleeved white shirt, its front buttons complaining at the workload imposed by the torso it contained.

'Yes. That's me.'

'Ah, *va bene*. You look like the picture they gave me.'

'You are my driver?'

'Yes, sir. I am very sorry I am late and missed you in the arrivals. Traffic. You will know all about traffic, coming from London.'

Luke assured him that it was fine, that he was in no rush. As well as there being nothing to grow anxious about, there was nothing to rush for any longer. His life was his own and there was a pleasure in suiting himself after so many years of being at the beck and call of others. The absence of commitments and obligations was one of the few comforts of his situation. He had made no arrangement to see the man he had come here to see, anyway. If he wasn't there tonight, Luke could find a little *pensione* in the village and try again tomorrow morning before going on to the hotel.

'And your name?' Luke asked.

'I am Giuseppe,' he said. 'Please call me Beppe.'

The driver gestured towards a black Mercedes parked just across the road and took Luke's suitcase. Well, it was Billie's really but better than any he owned, since she was a frequent and veteran traveller and had treated herself to it. Now it had become a reminder of her and a suitable companion on this trip. Beppe wheeled it across the road and deposited it in his boot, Luke retaining his shoulder bag and following a couple of steps behind. The driver opened a rear door for Luke, who removed his hat and settled into the soft leather of the back seat. Thankfully the air conditioning blew into life quickly after Beppe had switched on the car's ignition. Luke's stone-coloured linen suit was already crumpled, his blue cotton shirt damp with sweat.

As the car pulled out of the airport, past the bougainvillea baskets hanging from the lampposts, and headed north towards his destination in the hills about an hour away, a shard of apprehension pierced his stomach. Such stabs had been familiar for the first two years and he had grown accustomed to them. They had even become comfortable in their familiarity in his better moments. He hadn't felt one like this for a while, however. This one was sharper, rawer. What had seemed like an interesting idea composed in the safety of theory suddenly felt real. And very daunting. Yet, over the last few months, he had felt drawn back to fulfil this mission, to scratch an itch. Just as he had come to see in accepting everything about Billie – the intensity both demanding and rewarding at a time in his life when he had been hurt so badly and was reluctant to take a risk – Luke knew again now that there would be no peace until it was done.

2

His gaze out of the car window – at vistas by turns expansive and charming, revealed by the high viaducts or the dense flora and fauna on the climb away from the city – was interrupted by the darkness of the first tunnel through the hills. Pools of light from overhead punctuated the gloom and transported him back to the mists of that dank November late afternoon. It didn't take much to trigger the memory. It was the ninth. A Thursday. At 5.12pm. Some dates and times are forever branded on a psyche.

That day, like a creeping thief, the darkness snuck in and the church bells from the end of their road had not long stopped tolling as invitation to Evensong, the urgency a counterpoint to her breath growing shallower. The nurse had turned on two table lamps in corners of the room to provide pools of light.

'Would you like a light on back there?' came the voice from the front of the car. Luke turned his eyes from the blackened brickwork of the tunnel rushing past and saw the whites of Beppe's eyes in the rear-view mirror.

'I'm sorry?' said Luke.

'We will be going through many tunnels on the way. I thought maybe you'd like some light in the back.'

'What? Oh, no. Thank you.'

'Maybe you have something to read. Or write. I just thought… You know, Signor.'

'No. Nothing I want to read. And nothing to write. Nothing at all to write.'

He could see Beppe nod as they emerged from the tunnel back into the sunlight.

'We will be there in about thirty minutes,' said Beppe. A frisson of anxiety gnawed anew at Luke. The madness that had once inhabited him had finally retreated, even if he suspected it lurked in the undergrowth still. In England his desire to come here and make sense of competing states of confusion and ignorance had felt right. Now in Italy it seemed sheer folly and he felt himself ridiculous. Ridiculous and exposed. Ridiculous, exposed and vulnerable.

He had known about *him*, of course he had, but Luke had never really wanted to know too much about Billie's life before he met her. They'd talked occasionally and in passing about past loves but it seemed vicarious, even dangerous, to want to know any more detail or depth. She'd naturally had more partners than he had because she had been a single woman, but he had never really been interested in them, nor in the chronology of any encounters or relationships. That way, he believed, lay an insanity.

It was the discovery of the letters and the diaries that had stirred the mire in the fetid pond of his grief, plotting a new course in the passage of his mourning.

Billie's work when filming had taken her away for days, or even weeks, at a time but when temporarily on his own in the house, he had never felt inclined to explore the office that held her private world, nor to delve into the troves of its desk drawers, cupboards and filing cabinets. Partly that was because he trusted her – once they had met, they both realised they were each other's solution and neither wanted to do anything that would jeopardise that. Partly it was also that he was bound up in his own work and life. It was a different matter once the aloneness had become permanent; he had just not been able to resist. The curiosity of those who lament their lost loved one, casting haphazardly for information and answers and reasons, had swallowed his fevered obsession.

Here lay the chronicles and illustrations of a life in all its meticulous messiness. The teenage diaries had been amusing. Dark angst here and there, gloomy poems. Standard stuff of any self-respecting sixth-former about the pain of being unable to envisage a life beyond exam misery. The poetry was well written, though, even esoteric. He would have expected nothing less of Billie. Much more entertaining were the accounts of self-conscious nights out and awkward encounters with boys.

"Curry in the precinct with Lisa, Pete and Dave," she had written of one Saturday sixth-form night. "Should never have ordered the lamb vindaloo. But then the two pints of lager and 10 cigs probably didn't help. I don't think I'll be going out with Dave again. Can't say I blame him. Nobody likes being thrown up over when you're mid-snog, do they?"

Luke smiled. That sounded like Billie. She was funny, with self-awareness. Firmly in touch with life's excruciations. Seeing it written down that she had kissed somebody other than him did not, at that point, provoke any jealousy in him. It was long before he had known her, after all. The boy clearly meant nothing to her. No, those diaries were not what had stirred him up, invoked in him something terrifyingly, gaspingly visceral.

The photos – hundreds of them stowed away in a bottom drawer of the filing cabinet, ready to be stirred angrily from their slumbers – had begun his descent. They were of her life back between him and her first love, of smiling faces against sunny, coastal backdrops. Of short-lived ex-boyfriends, their right arms curled behind her neck, right hand emerging on her shoulder, her left arm around their waist. He had known she was a hoarder. That much was evident from all the clothes in her wardrobe that she had not worn for years but could not bear to dispose of. Just as he had been unable to since. But no, though he cursed her for never having sorted and sifted this heap of plastic wallets full of old photos, and though he would have preferred the ignorance of never seeing them, even then he wasn't overly discomforted by snapshots from relationships that clearly mattered at the time but had not enduringly fulfilled nor retained her. Only he had lasted. He should be grateful, he told himself, that those liaisons and episodes hadn't worked out.

It was, more, the box in the bottom drawer of her desk that had tipped him over the precipice from the melancholy into the madness. In normal circumstances, he would never have found it. On the odd occasion when he had actually ventured in to her office – to look for something, to borrow a stapler or paper clips perhaps – he wouldn't have lingered on the drawer, soon continuing his search elsewhere. At first glance, it simply looked to contain a transparent file of documents about her car. But now he had time on his hands and the whole house was his sole inheritance, as mitigation of pain, even if she did remain omnipresent, ever at his shoulder. He could mooch and meander, graze from room to room. Look wherever he chose and at his leisure. And when he idly lifted the file, there was the box.

It was wooden, a light wood, and plain. She could have chosen a similarly sized shoe box, but clearly what resided inside had some value, needed to be preserved and protected. Probably not significant value, however. Surely the box would have been more ornate if so? Hadn't she bought an expensive little art deco casket of light and dark wood for the engagement and wedding rings he had given her? Billie's sheaves of notebooks and papers were usually kept in tatty cardboard containers recycled from delivery companies. This box told of something meaningful to her and her life, but not with import enough for it to be treasured. At least that was what he tried to reason to himself later.

It was locked. What were the contents that required such concealment? He felt momentarily frustrated, wondering if it was a sign that he shouldn't pry. But then, the tiny key was easily located in a corner of the top drawer of the desk. Billie could be secretive, he remembered, but often couldn't be bothered to hide things too covertly. She was far too defiant for that. She'd always been able to explain herself by insisting black was white and bamboozling him if he confronted her about anything, leaving him feeling it was his fault for questioning her. What about that money she had been left by a dead aunt and never told him about until another relative let it slip in front of him? She'd used it to go to Namibia on her own... if indeed she did go on her own, his paranoia taunted him.

He inserted the key nervously, turned it to the thump of his increasing heartbeat. He paused. Did he really want to discover its contents? No, not really, he decided. Some things were best left alone. Undisturbed. But also yes. Yes, he did. He realised there was so much he didn't really know about her from her life before them. And he wanted to know. She was his wife, the woman he had loved above all. He wanted the other pieces of the puzzle that Billie had become to him all of a sudden. He wanted to join the dots of her life.

There must have been fifty letters inside the box and, underneath them, ten diaries covering the years of her life with *him*. The letters were tied in white ribbon. Not red, then. At least it wasn't the colour of love. He loosened the bow gently, with a mix of respect and trepidation, before staring at them momentarily, thinking again. He began to leaf slowly through them, as if flicking through LPs in the record shops of his youth. The envelopes were a mixture of air mail and ordinary white stationery, their postmarks varied, including a couple of English university cities, dated across five years. And then a final one, another five years later, out of context with the others. The handwriting on the front was the same each time, bearing the addresses of a couple of flats and houses he recognised as places Billie had told Luke she had worked after Birmingham University. Neatly, helpfully, they were in chronological order, dating back to her first year at uni.

He removed the letter on the bottom of the pile first, most curious about what had made it the last, teasing it carefully from its slit envelope, as if examining a delicate historical document. He wondered if he should be wearing white cotton gloves. He wanted first to check the signature. It was the one he was expecting. The material was incendiary, that bottom letter the bitter end of a relationship.

The address on the top envelope was a small town in Switzerland. Luke began to access information from long-ago conversations, when he and Billie were new to each other, in those flirty, exciting early moments of a relationship when each wants avidly to hear of the other's present and past but neither wants to venture anything damaging that might deter the other and end something before it had started. He'd told her of his separation from Jane a year previously, his divorce eight months after that. He recalled Billie telling of her own one long-term relationship. Of meeting *him* in her first term at Birmingham, he a researcher in a science programme, eight years older than her. He remembered too her working abroad at the end of the first year. Helping on a farm wasn't it? Years ago, of course. No threat or danger. Ancient history.

"My dearest Billie," the first letter began somewhat formally, going on to hope that she was enjoying being with her friend Lisa, and that the work was going well. It was newsy, chatty and surprisingly lacking in intimacy. But then these were students, one current, one not too long before, and not given to soppiness, Luke supposed. They'd probably only been apart a few weeks since the end of term. He'd gone to her diaries then, checking the entries for the days around those two letters, top and bottom, first and last.

The feel of the car slowing brought him back to the here and now. They were coming off the autostrada, down into a valley.

'We are near now,' said Beppe. The road from the roundabout snaked and hairpinned its way up to the village, past oak and chestnut trees, past an olive grove, to a plateau at the top of a hill. It was a village that Luke felt he knew much about, despite it being his first visit, having read all he could find on the internet.

'The company told me only the name of the village. Campaglia,' said Beppe. 'They did not give me an address. So where would you like me to take you?'

'Just to the piazza,' said Luke. 'Park up please and wait for me.'

Beppe did as he was asked and they were soon in the square. This was a small place, where all roads led to the commercial centre, such as it was, in the piazza. There was a little market here each day, selling fruit and vegetables and cheap clothing, but the few traders left were clearing up now, it being late afternoon. The Mercedes attracted the odd glance, as did the man who emerged from the back of the car and put on his hat and sunglasses.

Hit by the punch of heat that the day was not yet ready to cede, Luke stood for a moment taking in the few shops and businesses surrounding the square: a small supermarket, a pizzeria, a bar. And a church, a fussy, ornate little church, the Chiesa San Marco. He recognised them all from the village's website. He had pictured himself here many times and had worked out his plan, though it could only ever be tentative, relying as it did on the co-operation of others. To have tried to engineer this another way by asking permission risked complete failure. At least this way he was taking action and stood some chance of achieving his goal. Luke reasoned that people were more likely to agree to things in person than via a tag on social media, or a phone call or email, even if he could have acquired numbers or addresses.

He went to the boot of the car and took out his shoulder bag before walking across to the bar, *Il Assetate*. He was certainly thirsty enough for refreshment after the journey. It was that time between the end of afternoon work and the start of evening activity, when the climate induced a lassitude, and the bar was quiet. The bistro tables outside were empty and so the proprietor was quickly with him when Luke installed himself in a white plastic chair.

'Si Signor?' said the man in his forties. His tone was not as welcoming as Luke had hoped.

'*Un doppio espresso e un'acqua minerale frizzante, per favore,*' Luke replied.

'You like ice with the water?' the man asked.

'My accent is that bad, then?' Luke said.

The man smiled. 'They will be with you momentarily.'

'Thank you. *Grazie.*'

'*Prago.*'

Luke looked across to the car, where Beppe was scrolling through his phone, then scanned the square. There was just one man left, returning unsold produce to the back of his Fiat mini pick-up. A couple of old women waddling home with bags of shopping. Luke wondered what might happen, how he might react, if *he* walked across the square now. A shudder went through him as he contemplated his mission.

The barman returned with his order and set it down.

'Thank you, er...'

'Filippo,' said the man.

'Thank you Filippo.'

"You are welcome."

'This is a beautiful village.'

'Yes, it is.'

'Are you from here?'

'I own this bar. It was my father's before and I have lived here my whole life. Apart from a year in England as a young man.'

'Which is why your English is so good.'

Filippo shrugged. 'I followed a woman, you know…'

Yes, Luke replied, he did know. This man might understand something, then, about quests.

The barman smiled, easing Luke's anxiety that others might be hostile when he explained what he was doing here.

'I wonder if you would sit with me for a few minutes,' Luke enquired. 'Perhaps let me buy you a drink?'

'OK,' said Filippo. 'I will take a cola. Thank you.'

He went inside and brought his drink back with him, sitting opposite Luke. There was a moment of silence as Luke drew a hit of coffee, followed by a cleansing mouthful of mineral water.

'I am guessing there is something you would like to ask me, Mr…'

'Jessop. Luke Jessop.'

'So how can I help you, Luke Jessop? We don't get many English people up here. They stay more at the coast. I am right – you are seeking something, yes?'

Luke reached into the inside pocket of his jacket and brought out a photo that he had found in the deep drawer in Billie's office. He slid it across the table and Filippo bent over to take it in, though only briefly. It was clear he recognised the smiling face in the close-up portrait lit by a foreign sun. He looked up at Luke.

'What is it you want with this man?'

'You know him, then?'

'Of course. He lives in this village. But I am guessing you know that already.'

And of course Luke did. He had found Adam Byrne easily enough on social media and his profiles had showed his location – the village, that was, but not the actual address.

'What do you want with him?' Filippo pressed.

'Just to speak with him.'

'Does he owe you money?'

'No, nothing like that. In fact, I have something for him.'

Luke reached down and picked up his shoulder bag from the foot of his seat. He tapped it.

'Mr Jessop. I hope you will forgive me for being a little suspicious. Adam has lived in our community for some time now and we respect him. When a stranger comes and asks for him... Well, I hope you would see how you might react if somebody came asking for a friend of yours in the place where you lived.'

Luke nodded. He did take Filippo's point. Nobody, he thought, sees themselves as sinister but at this moment he acknowledged he must have looked that way. Just as he had guessed that the bar owner would be the fount of all village knowledge, he had prepared for such a reaction and decided that honesty, if it had been limited initially, was going to be the best policy.

'Look, I know this might sound a little unusual but I just have something I want to discuss with Mr Byrne. We have – had – a mutual friend and... well, it's sort of important to me.'

He looked Filippo directly in the face and the man looked straight back at him. There was a silence between the two of them as they each probed the authenticity in each other's eyes. Luke thought that Filippo must have seen pathos in his, as well as a pleading sincerity in his voice. 'Do I look weird to you?' he asked. 'Or dangerous?'

After a moment, Filippo spoke. 'No, I guess not,' he said. 'But there is something I do not understand... You have found the village where Adam lives. Why did you not find his address? Write to him. Arrange a meeting.'

'I did look on the internet,' Luke replied. 'But I couldn't find an actual address. His social media showed his location and some pictures of his life here but nothing more.'

Luke looked across the square, buying himself some time before considering how to deliver what he had been thinking and rehearsing. He saw Beppe reclining in the driver's seat, napping.

'And, to be honest,' Luke continued, 'I didn't really want to write to him because... well, I wanted to be spontaneous. I didn't know how I would feel until I got here. I thought I might just have second thoughts and if I'd made an appointment, I would be letting him down. Anyway I am on the way to a short holiday in Recoli and I thought I could kill two birds with one stone.'

'We are less cruel in Italy,' Filippo said. 'We say "to catch two pigeons with one bean."' He smiled and Luke could not help but smile himself. There was another silence. Still, Filippo was giving nothing away.

'OK, look,' said Luke, realising that he was going to have to reveal his whole hand rather than lay down one card at a time 'Here's the thing. My wife died almost three years ago now. Adam Byrne was her first lover and some months after she died I found letters from him to her that she had kept. I felt drawn to meet him. To talk to him about a woman with whom we clearly shared a love, a woman who still dominates my life though she is no longer physically in it. To have a conversation in person. I have spoken to so many who knew her. I want to know everything about her as I met her only later in life. Mr Byrne may be able to help me in my need to know more. And I want to return the letters to him. Also in person.'

Filippo was silent for a moment. 'The bag...'

'Yes, the letters are in a box in this bag.'

Filippo nodded and looked around the square. He took a swig of his cola and rolled it in his mouth, savouring it, Luke watching every movement of his face for signs of his intent. At last, Filippo answered.

'OK, Luke Jessop. I am very sorry for your loss. I believe you and I think I understand.' He pointed to an arch in the corner of the square. 'You see there? Go under the arch into Via Bettolo. You will find Adam at number sixteen.'

Luke finished his espresso and stood, laying a generous twenty Euro note on the table. He offered a hand, which Filippo rose to shake.

'Thank you. I am most grateful,' said Luke and headed for Via Bettolo immediately, lest he lose courage. He mused, not for the first time in the last two years and more, how the mention of a deceased wife, as with the utterance of the word cancer, immediately changed people's attitudes. He did not feel guilty, however. He had told the truth, been honest. People, he was sure, could scent honesty as much as they could sniff deceit.

Via Bettolo was a narrow street that no cars could access. Either side of the cobbled walkway stood charming terraced three-storey houses, many clad in ivy and bougainvillea. An elderly man, his expansive stomach bare and tanned, sat outside his front door on a chair that was threatening to collapse underneath him. He watched suspiciously Luke's every step as he passed but issued a '*buonasera*,' that Luke returned.

Within a couple of minutes, Luke stood before the solid olive green door of number sixteen. He noticed the beads of sweat on the bone of his brow, and his heart racing, an echo of that first date with Billie. Her voice and smile, both welcome and intrusive, appeared to him. *What's the worst that can happen?* Luke imagined her saying. He sensed that she would have liked the prospect of two men, two who had loved her, talking about her. *Only one thing worse than being talked about...* she might well have said.

He tugged at a long iron rod to the side of the door and heard a bell sound inside. He looked nervously up and down the street. Nothing, nobody, was moving. And then with a long creak, the door opened. A bearded man stood looking him up and down, bemusement on his face.

'*Sì?*'

'Adam Byrne?'

The man eyed him with suspicion.

'Yes… You're English, right? I don't think I know you.' Byrne's accent was Irish. Luke remembered now that Billie had mentioned he was from Dublin.

'My name is Luke Jessop.'

'It doesn't mean anything to me. I'm sorry…'

'I was married to Billie. Billie Forrester.'

Byrne looked horrified. His tone became brusque. 'Billie. My God.'

'You two were together for quite a while, I think.'

'That was a long time ago. Look, what do you want?'

'Just to talk. Maybe to reminisce.'

Byrne looked up towards the square and the arch at the top of Via Bettolo. Anxiety creased his face.

'Look. Leave me alone. I have nothing to say to you. Especially, I don't wish to talk to you about Billie.'

'She died. Almost three years ago.'

'She did? Well, I'm sorry about that. And sorry for you. But there's an end to it."

'I have something I thought you might like to see.'

'What?'

Luke swung the shoulder bag to the ground, unzipped it and produced the box.

'Letters. These are letters I found. They're from you to her. She kept them.'

'Bloody hell. No. I don't want them. Now go, please.'

'Listen, she was, still is, precious to me. I'm guessing she once was to you. We share something. Something significant. I just thought…'

At that moment, Luke heard the sound of footsteps on the cobbles coming from the direction of the square. He turned to see a woman walking towards them. Turning his gaze back to Byrne, he saw eyes betraying panic.

'Go. Just go. And take the bloody letters with you.'

'Well, I'm sorry… Listen, if you'd ever like to speak to me, here's my number.'

Luke took a business card from his wallet and tried to hand it over but Byrne refused to take it.

'OK,' Luke added. 'If you do change your mind, I'll be at the Hotel Miramare in Recoli for the next few days. I loved her and so did you once. I just thought maybe…'

Suddenly the woman had arrived alongside them.

'Who is this, Adam?'

'I'll explain when he's gone, Christine. And he's just going, aren't you, Mr Jessop?'

Luke nodded slowly. He picked up the bag, turned and trudged slowly away. When he looked back, halfway up Via Bettolo, Byrne and the woman had gone inside. He sensed the conversation between them was going to be difficult and he felt uneasy. What had he expected, intruding on not just one life, but two, both of whom occupied a different world from his, even if there had once been a bridge between them?

He stood still for a moment to take stock before reaching the square. 'Fuck it. Fuck IT. FUCK IT,' he bellowed with increasing volume. He heard a window open above him and looked up to see the old man previously sitting on the chair looking down on him. Embarrassed, Luke hurried away.

Once in the square, a tristesse enveloped him, replacing his anger. Grief was part of it, yes, but that uneasiness, he discerned now, was shame. He had been selfish, imagined that his feelings as the bereaved husband were paramount and that everyone would understand that and accommodate him. He hadn't thought enough about the feelings of others, of Byrne in particular. Certainly not those of his Christine.

He looked at his watch. It was just before five o'clock. The bells of San Marco began to toll, calling the villagers to vespers to give thanks for the day. He roused Beppe from his nap and asked him to drive as quickly as these narrow, snaking roads out of the village would allow.

3

As his eyes opened, Luke was immediately confronted by the empty space alongside him. It was a familiar sight but in an unfamiliar location, or at least one he had not been to for just over three years. One day, people said, there would come a time when his first thought of the day was not her. Today was not that day. He looked at his watch. It was 6.33am. He sat up in the double bed and looked across to the tall windows. He remembered having opened one last night as the evening and the room were still warm. Now the thin floral cotton curtain billowed in the sea breeze. The view from the balcony beckoned him.

He'd arrived at dusk the previous evening, exhausted, both physically by the trip and emotionally by the encounter with Adam Byrne. His shame – the guilt of having disturbed Byrne graduating to disgust with himself at his crassness – was debilitating. Guilt was an all too familiar feeling from the first two angst-infused years without Billie. Since her death, he had berated himself for so much that he should have done better. He could, should, have travelled with her more, watched more films with her, more often massaged her feet, which ached from the chemotherapy, when she asked him. He should have shown her more physical affection in the seventeen years of their marriage but he had been afraid of making himself too vulnerable and it hurting all the more when they argued.

In the aftermath of her death, he had wanted so many times to start again, to do it all differently this time, without conflict but knowing instead that they were, eventually, going to survive adversities together, rather than bolt from each other. Given a second opportunity, he would not take their life together for granted. Familiarity and the casualness with each other that it brought, however, was the fate of partners who slipped into their togetherness.

Grief uncovered such thoughts, exposed such regret. It found every little vent, every nook and cranny, into heart and soul, where it could wreak its havoc, touch each nerve, find every sore point and bastard vulnerability. Sometimes he was angry with her for putting him through this pain and exposing all of his insecurities. Sometimes, idealising the past and idolising her, he felt he loved her more since she'd died, since the realities of relationships, the resentments, no longer intruded on the silence of his life now. It had seemed simplistic to him in the past when people referred to their partners as 'my other half', but he recognised its truth now. She was the other half of the bed, of the conversation, of the meal table.

On his arrival at the hotel, he'd not been able to face a dining room alone and so had ordered an omelette and a glass of milk from room service. Within an hour of eating it, he had drifted into a fitful sleep punctuated by the demands of a sixty-year-old prostate and the awakening from a regular dream in which he was unable to find his car, dashing hither and thither in panic, discovering it was at none of the locations where he thought he had left it.

Whereas during the night he had been so tired that he knew he would fall back into some sort of slumber – however short it might be – after these interruptions, now he knew for sure he would not get back to sleep. He looked across to the balcony and pictured her there as before, naked, draining every drop from the view. Her slender back and narrow shoulders, her snake hips. He had told her to come away from the window, that somebody below would be able to see her breasts. *'Oh for God's sake Luke. Don't be such a prude,'* she'd said. He had smiled at her, at that moment.

Unable to endure the intense beauty of the memory, or the vacancy at his side, he rose and drew back the curtains. The sun was rising to its task of illuminating the ravishing view that she had taken in on this very spot. As he watched, enthralled, sunlight minute by minute laid yellow petals on the Ligurian sea on its path to the horizon. To his left stood the cliffs that concealed the cove where the monastery of San Pietro looked down on what had been their favourite beachside restaurant, but to which he was now dubious about returning given the poignancy of that final visit that returned to his mind's eye. Beyond that lay the small towns of the Cinque Terre. To his right was Recoli, part seaside resort, part small fishing town, with the Basilica San Prospero on the promontory dividing the shingled beach and picturesque harbour. Immediately beneath his room, there awaited an azure saltwater swimming pool surrounded by palms and wooden sunbeds topped with red and white striped cushions.

They had always booked this room on the third floor every year after their first visit for this very view – not too high should the lift not be working and they needed to take the stairs, not too low to be close to the noise of the pool area. And the first thing they had done after checking in was to dash here, drop the suitcases and consume this panorama as with a first invigorating gulp of strong coffee in the morning. He had looked only casually out of the window last night in the twilight, closed to its splendour. He was not only tired but troubled still by the encounter with Byrne, was picking over its bones. Enough of that this morning. He was sure his cheeks would burn with the naïve audacity of his detour to Campaglia again some time, and probably very soon, but enough was enough for now. It was a gorgeous new morning promising heat, and the memory of Billie had seized centre stage. Whatever was occupying him would always be sidelined in her death as it had been in her life. She was just a centre-stage kind of gal.

Luke had adored this place, but then that was with her. He wondered if he still would or could. A few months back, he had finally decided that he was at least been willing to find out, prompted by an article he had read about the value of pilgrimage for the bereaved. Returning to significant locations that had meant so much, it said, could bring new meanings to the memories of one who had been lost. Such had been the pain and the introspection of the first two years that he had been unable to see any life outside his immediate environment, needing the safety and control of being at the hub of his own territory. Not that he was alone in it. He was still enveloped by her and the ornaments that she had bought, furniture she had chosen. Here, now, as with visiting Byrne, at least he was taking some sort of action for himself, opening up to new thoughts and feelings. The temptation since her death had been to create a sealed world, where there may have been pain but it was a pain that became familiar and regular enough to make it hard for new pain to intrude.

There was still half an hour before the dining room opened for breakfast and so he decided on a walk to stimulate his appetite. And now that Billie had demanded his attention anew, he wanted to retread their movements around the town as soon as possible. Not all of it now, for there were three full days still to gather up those movements and their memories – as well as a task to perform on the final evening – but he wanted to make a start and feel their sweet piquancy, like astringent lotion on a shaving cut.

He donned shorts, polo shirt, trainers and sunglasses, took the stairs and made his way through the marbled lobby of the Miramare. From the square in front of the hotel, he turned left, down a narrow alley hemmed in by elegant terraced apartment blocks of pink, terracotta and yellow, with *trompe-l'oeil* windows painted onto them, and washing hanging over balconies. It had been one of the things she had liked. Recoli was earthier, more native, than the more expensive towns along the coast often overrun by tourists. He remembered well-read Billie quoting Camus at him, talking of the Mediterranean having a "triumphant taste for life."

'Italians come here on holiday,' she'd also said. 'Always a good sign.'

'Like seeing Chinese people in Chinese restaurants,' Luke had replied. 'Trouble is with an Italian resort like this you want to find another one a few hours later.'

She had rolled her eyes and tutted but also smiled. A smile from such a demanding audience was compliment indeed. He loved to amuse her, knew it was part of what had attracted her, and kept her attracted (unlike with the men of her earlier life, whose charm had faded once the physical attraction had worn off). Even though they'd been together for years, she liked him continuing to be funny, or trying to be, outside his writing room. The subtext was that she was worth it, even more than those who paid him to be funny. Or did then. Nobody did now.

The alley opened up on to the *lungomare* and he stopped awhile, his breath taken again by that sea, that bluest of seas, with the sun now risen to illuminate its splendour. They had paused here together those first mornings on each of their four annual visits, falling in love again with the moment each time; savouring the prospect of a week walking this promenade, feeling these sensations. *'Another bloody week in paradise,'* she always said. It was ritual and comforting. For at least eighteen months after her death, Luke's memories had been double-edged – solace, yes, but jagged reminders of what was lost. Thankfully, this morning's were gentle and he was relieved. There was promise of warmth and progress, though he dared not yet believe that he was free of any retreat to cold comfort.

It was not a beautiful beach. The stones of the public areas were grey and not as welcoming as the sand of Sta Margherita Ligure a few miles away. But the colours of the private, roped-off sections, their matching sun loungers and parasols of blues and reds and yellows and greens, in stripes and hoops, were jolly and cheering. He passed by each closed souvenir shop and ice cream parlour as if walking by the beds of a dormitory of old acquaintances still asleep. There, dormant still, was her favourite one – the little bookshop, with its trestle table of English-language books outside when open. She had always been amused that the mafia and camorra had a whole section to themselves.

Upon reaching the church, he found a bench where he could sit down to drink from its fountain of sights, as they had done that first morning. He didn't yet want to press on to the harbour, as the snapshots and video clips of her were gushing into his brain and he wanted to hold some back for later, unwilling to let them dilute the images currently enfolding him. For now, he needed solitude and to be sedentary just to process them all. The pleasure on her face as she tasted that first sip of white wine before dinner, or her grin as she took a long lick of *stracciatella* ice cream with long, languid tongue. Those yelps of pain as she tried to traverse the stones barefoot for a paddle in the sea, he laughing and refusing to bring her shoes to her. Of course he'd relented. The picture in his mind suddenly became too much. The sadness of what was lost edged ahead of the gratitude for what he had found. He cast his eye around for diversion.

There were few people about this early in the morning. Seaside resorts woke late after evenings extended to facilitate the spending of money. The fishing boats were already out. Luke saw a woman walk purposefully from the direction of the harbour towards his bench. She looked to be around his age, he noted as she neared. She wore a ghastly, gaudy pink velour tracksuit and matching trainers. Her red hair was tied into a ponytail.

'*Buongiorno*,' she said and smiled widely, not stopping.

'*Buongiorno*,' he replied, offering only a curt smile in return.

Luke watched her stride off on what looked like a determined effort to start the day with a significant contribution to her step count. He was assailed by a vision of Billie struggling to walk near the end, a stick taking her dwindling weight until she finally succumbed and submitted, grumbling, to the wheelchair. He looked at his watch. 7.30am. The dining room would be open for breakfast, and he was hungry now. He would go back to the room to shower and change. The temperature was already in the low-twenties, he guessed.

As he crossed the reception area of the hotel, he heard a call of 'Signor Jessop.' He turned to see Massimo, the hotel's manager walking towards him and offering a warm handshake.

'We were all so terribly sorry to hear of the passing of your wife,' said Massimo.

'Thank you for emailing me those pictures,' Luke replied.

'Well, we were most grateful for you sending the money. The staff were only too happy to do as you requested and toast Signora Billie with Champagne on the terrace.'

'She loved that terrace.'

Massimo smiled. 'We all remember her with fondness.'

'Once met, never forgotten,' added Luke.

'Exactly. We are so happy that you have felt able to return and stay with us again. I do hope your room is as comfortable as you remember.'

'And as beautiful, yes, thank you. How has your season been?'

'Very good, yes. The weather has been very hot. Good for business but not so great for the staff, perhaps. Too dry, also. No rain for three months. Our region, our agriculture, need some now. We will be glad when we have the rainwaters.'

'Well, maybe after the next few days. Sorry that sounds very selfish, doesn't it?'

'Signor Jessop, after what you have experienced, I think you may be permitted some selfishness.'

Luke was touched. 'Thank you, Massimo,' he said. 'Now, one of your spectacular breakfasts, I think.'

Massimo smiled again and Luke made his way back to his room to shower. As the water gushed, he felt a tear falling from his eye. Soon more came, then a torrent of them accompanied by a guttural sound of choked pain. He pressed his hands into the shower wall, bowed his head and felt the water cascade down his back. He remembered her back. So slim, so smooth, so perfect. Until the cancer drugs demanded payment for their work and caused a huge black bruise at its centre. Like a target. He stood weeping, for how long he knew not. Until he grew tired of his tears.

In slow motion, he readied himself for the dining room, this time donning a long-sleeved blue linen shirt, chinos and brown leather deck shoes. After such a session of sadness, it always helped to dress properly, he felt. It was a sign that he could still take care of himself, was determined not to return to the mess, both physical and emotional, of those early days and months. He recalled his long-dead father, a civil servant; as long as he could put on a shirt and tie and go to work each morning, all was well and any personal issues could be postponed. While Luke did not believe in permanent denial, he accepted that the temporary protection it afforded was valuable at times.

He was relieved that Franco, the maître d', did not make a fuss beyond a shake of the hand and a 'Welcome back, Signor Jessop.' Massimo would probably have had a word with the staff to keep things low key. Luke liked that. It was an expensive hotel for good reason, not just because of its furnishings and facilities, or its location; its well-trained staff and discretion added to its value for money. '*You get what you pay for,*' she'd said. And she was right. She always was. Even when she was wrong.

Franco showed him to a table in the window, with another splendid view of the hotel's small private beach at the foot of the cliff on which it was built. Very quickly a waiter came to take his order for coffee. The attentiveness shown towards the grieving as soon as people knew of their bereavement was one slither of consolation for which he was grateful. There had to be some consolations as counterpoint to the penetration of the pain, didn't there? His coffee duly arrived swiftly, not just because the airy room, scene of so many wedding receptions that they had observed and smiled at down the years, was no more than a third full at this late stage of the season. The waiting and kitchen staff, he was sure, would by now know who he was. And what had happened to him.

('Take advantage of it,' a comedy-show director who had taken him out for lunch a few months after Billie's death had said to him. 'You get a free pass for a fair old while. You can do, say, and ask for anything. Nobody will bat an eyelid and everybody will do anything they can for you.' The guy had then asked if Luke minded paying as he was a little short right now – and then laughed at the shock on Luke's face before picking up the bill.)

Luke sipped the coffee and remembered the first time he and Billie had taken breakfast here. '*Oh my God,*' she had said. '*Is that not just the best coffee you've ever tasted?*' He had been thinking the same thing and smiled at her. They'd been ready for caffeine after that early-morning stroll to get their bearings and explore their new surroundings. Just as he was now ready for new energy after his own evocative walk this morning.

As he drained the first cup, he looked around the room. No children, just couples. They all seemed to come from an age range between the parents of children now at university and the moneyed retired from prosperous parts of Europe. Over there, two tanned Teutons, possibly a BMW dealer from Baden-Baden and his well-coiffured wife. Both were dressed in what were clearly designer clothes and oozed money. Beyond them a Swedish couple probably. They looked so healthy and beautifully co-ordinated in expensive light denim. Even their blonde hair had faded to grey in unison. Car industry ad directors in search of the grey pound would have cast the harmonious couple as soon as they walked into the room. Meanwhile, in the corner those were clearly two Brits. He bald, she pinched of face, they looked as if they had been bickering already as they stared silently in opposite directions.

That woman over there on her own... was that not the woman who had said '*buongiorno*' to him this morning? Her flame hair, released from its ponytail tie, was still wet from showering and now, instead of that hideous pink velour tracksuit, she was wearing a neat green shift dress. Billie had had one similar. The woman was smiling. The bronzed man at the table next to her, with his handsome, angular features framed by wavy salt-and-pepper grey hair, had clearly said something funny to her and she was amused.

Luke rose and fetched himself a cross section of the generous buffet, at its centre a plate of scrambled egg and speck bacon. As always here. It would set him up for a day of stretching out on a sunbed by the pool, with book, crossword and earphones to hand. He watched the affluent Germans, the elegant Swedes and the dishevelled Brits leave while he lingered over his second pot of coffee. He also noted the red-headed woman leave and looked across at the salt-and-pepper man, who was also eyeing her departure. Luke left soon afterwards himself, pausing to take in the large landscape painting that hung at the dining room's entrance. It was a jolly, colourful scene of Felliniesque figures caricatured from the back, their legs elongated, their backsides broad. They were looking out from the terrace of the hotel on to a bustling Recoli beach with all its parasols unfurled. A beam came to his face. Billie had loved it. Viewing it on the way in to breakfast had always been a cheerful start to the day.

Back in his room, Luke recalled how the days acquired a rhythm when they came here. Some reading and resting before a swim in the pool, always on the cusp of refreshing and warm, when the sun reached its zenith. A languid lunch on the terrace; some fresh pasta with just-caught clams or prawns followed by a panna cotta. An afternoon of similar indolence interrupted only by an afternoon pot of tea with nibbles of crispy focaccia crackers.

After that, a nap perhaps, then a shower before a walk and an aperitif at that quiet bar at the end of the harbour. A few nights of the week, they would have dinner on the hotel's elegant terrace, where they would watch the sun go down over Genoa and the hills to the west as they ate. There would be some delicate fish usually followed by sumptuous desserts that would require abstinence when back home. They would take a brandy maybe in the bar before lying in bed and poking fun at an Italian game show on TV, presented by ageing male lotharios and blonde female sidekicks of cavernous cleavage. Cancer treatment had caused a corporeal lockdown for Billie but there could still be tender lovemaking and intimacy, before they fell asleep to the whisper of the sea through the open window, the sensation of the breeze and the scent of the cypresses.

At least that was how it developed as the week progressed. For the first day or two he struggled to give himself to the soothing regimen – unlike Billie who longed for it and wrapped herself in the comfort blanket it offered. He scrolled his phone, to her annoyance, checking his messages and emails. He wrote down anything he overheard or thought he could use in his work. Wondered how the show could survive without him. Worried that it would.

All that was gone, however, and he had little to do now but surrender to being single. The agenda for today sounded idyllic, and indeed he knew that his life was superficially a fortunate one, with its legacy of material comfort courtesy of pension funds and acquiring Billie's half of their monies. While he felt that he often lived in a dark room, he was thankful at least it was well furnished. Being lucky was not necessarily to feel lucky, however. There was a giant void at the centre of the ease his finances provided, and he still doubted that he would ever be ready to relax into his circumstances. Widowhood dominated him, he felt. He didn't know where he was in the stations of grief but he felt that the terminus – if there was some destination – was still a long way down the tracks.

To stretch on a sunbed was to hear her asking him to rub cream on to her back. Sitting alone at lunch was to picture the sensuous circle formed by her lips as it slurped a slither of linguine, a sensuous image also coming to him of a Valentine's Day card from years ago that she had sent him, featuring inside an imprint of a similar O of red-lipsticked mouth. And to order afternoon tea was to remember the first time they had taken it here together.

'Funny how I would want scones with cream and jam on holiday at home. Not here.' she'd said.

'What about Genoa cake instead?' Luke had replied and she'd smiled. 'In fact, Genoa'm surprised they've not thought of that.'

'You should write that one down,' she'd said and he did. It had gone into the rejected pile in the writers' room amid groans.

As the lazy day wore on, he found being back at this hotel on his own was like once again facing all the 'firsts' of the newly bereaved, the anniversaries and birthdays and memories that contained so many echoes of mourning. He was revisiting a precious place but one that was starting already to become unnerving after less than twenty-four hours here. Anxiety frequently fluttered in his stomach, restlessness infusing his limbs. He began to fear a return of the madness of the first year when his home, her office and its contents, had been a mine-field of unknowns. He had come here to pay homage to her and honour their life together, but the rebuff from Adam Byrne yesterday was a ramrod reminder of his aloneness out here.

He wondered if he might get a flight home tomorrow morning. Yes, good idea. This trip was a mistake. Did he really think that Byrne was just going to 'hail fellow, well met' him and ask him in to shoot the breeze about Billie? That revisiting this place where he and she had always been happy together, leaving at home the cares of a work-stressed couple, wasn't going to bring on the bitterness of loss to banish the sweetness of reminiscence? Anyway, it was just too bloody hot. Mid-September and thirty-three degrees? He'd spent much of the day in the shade, dipping into the pool occasionally for respite, lowering himself in sharply to conceal as quickly as possible his white body, comfort-fed by grief as well as greed.

He returned to his room to check flight availability on his laptop but something stopped him from pressing a 'Book Now' icon. He had come this far, he reminded himself, been through worse than this. This was all just an echo chamber of early grief. He had experienced and learned enough to know that he should not give in to his discomfort. Much as he may have wanted to escape his pain, he knew now that the only way through it was through it. There could be no circumvention if relief was to be lasting. And anyway, he was only here for three more nights. A long weekend but a short period in what was one of her favourite phrases, "the grand scheme of things".

Instead, he lay on the bed, luxuriating in the coolness of the room as the open windows funnelled the breeze in his direction, his anxiety abating as he heard her: *It's OK. Relax. It's what you came here for. You know you love it in this place. Come here, come to me...*

When he awoke from a nap, he realised that the sun had gone down and he was just fifteen minutes from his dinner reservation. He threw cold water across his face and put on a clean shirt and his chinos before hurrying down to the terrace restaurant. Sat at his table, he wondered why he had rushed. The place was half empty. But then punctuality was his nature and Billie also hated lateness. Old behaviour still ruled him though there was no call for haste in his life these days. The peace that had been hard won since, and which accompanied his arrival in Italy yesterday, was ebbing away. Perhaps he'd check that flight availability again before bed.

Of this morning's gathering, he could now see only the suave Scandinavians daintily dissecting fish. Oh, and flame-haired woman, this time with salt-and-pepper guy at her table over there, the lights of the city flickering behind them in the distance. He observed them for a while. The bloke seemed to think himself an amusing sort, laughing after saying something. He was certainly attentive. She seemed to have mixed feelings and reactions, smiling at times, insouciant at others. At one point, she looked across at Luke while he was staring in their direction – she even seemed to smile at him – but he looked swiftly back down at the menu.

He declined a starter of pasta so that he could have a dessert and ordered the meal they had both loved and which he had been dreaming and drooling about: sea bass in the Ligurian style, with olives, pine kernels and sweet tomatoes, sautéed potatoes and green beans on the side, accompanied by a half bottle of the house white. By the time of the tiramisu, the newly coupled-up pair had departed, the man shepherding her from the room with a hand in the small of her back. Luke couldn't deny that she looked attractive, in a white cotton dress with blue cardigan draped over her shoulders, but he could neither shake that vision of the velour tracksuit and matching pink trainers from his head nor judge her accordingly.

He sat there drinking a coffee for as long as he could before the self-consciousness of the lone diner finally bored him. He wondered if he would ever get used to it. He felt less conspicuous these days, but in formal dining rooms he still couldn't help wondering if people were considering his situation. He knew, more realistically, that nobody really cared about him, largely because they were more interested in themselves, but the opportunity for overthinking presented by solitude often deceived one into self-absorption.

Passing through the reception area, Luke saw the flame-haired woman and her new beau at ease over a nightcap as a pianist played *Claire de Lune*, but he did not let his gaze linger, unwilling to allow his vicarious interest to be piqued again, let alone noticed. He went straight to his room and lay in bed. He soon regretted having had the nap earlier as he stared at the fan on the high ceiling. Darkness always invited in the triggers of trauma, the visions of her on her death bed after a week of deterioration, the hollow cheeks, the expiration. Luke hadn't wept then. There had been a wearied acceptance to him in that precise moment. He'd had plenty of time to prepare and had imagined many times during that final year what it would be like. He'd pictured himself collapsing into paroxysms of pain, emitting uncontrollable sobs. But he did neither. Instead, he was overcome by a lassitude. He had given everything that last week of her dying and was spent.

'I shouldn't have gone to see Adam, Billie. I'm really sorry,' he said out loud, tears filling his eyes. 'I feel like I've betrayed you and your memory because of my own insecurities. Intruding on a life that was private to you. I just felt compelled to find out more about the woman I loved, that was all. You understand that, don't you? And coming here…? This was our place, not my place. I should have booked that flight home. I will tomorrow…'

Sshh. Sshh. Rest. Sleep. Give it a chance. We'll take a little walk by the harbour tomorrow. You always liked it by the harbour, didn't you? All will be well. And all manner of things will be well.

My dearest Billie,

How is life down on the farm? Or should it be up on the farm where you are? I have visions of you cupping an ear and listening out for cowbells in the foothills of the Alps trying to round up a stray Daisy for the night. Are you doing the milking in the morning? Do you have to get up at 5am? Is it all just like The Sound of Music?

Sorry to bombard you with questions but it would be good to hear from you. You usually send a postcard as soon as you get somewhere. Must be pretty busy there though, I suppose. Early starts, late finishes, I imagine. Would just like to know how you're getting on. It's not that I worry about you, as I know you're a strong, independent and capable woman, as you continually tell me. It's just that I'm interested in you, what you're doing and the life out there.

The campus has been quiet without all the undergrads around the place. Without the buzz, nobody seems to get much done in research departments. We all miss the energy. I thought I'd go home to Bray for a week to catch up with the folks and got here Saturday. Got the boat to Dún Laoghaire. I do admire the old man for building up his business, and his belief that he's at the heart of his community, but doing the same thing day in, day out would drive me nuts. Selling fruit and veg is genuinely a public service but it feels so dull to me.

It's weird also catching up with guys I was at school with. All of your school friends will be still in their teens and basically doing the same thing – at uni, sowing their wild oats (do women do that, or is it just blokes?) – but men in their mid-twenties are all over the place. Dermot, who you met when he came to Birmingham that weekend, is about to get married. John already is, and with a kid. Liam is working all hours all over the region as a sales rep. Getting them all together for a Guinness one evening is bloody hard work, I can tell you. I do think I've grown out of all this, my old mates and this town. Maybe I'll see if any of the old Trinity crowd are around in Dublin later in the week.

I've also come away from Brum to think. We're going to have to talk about what happens to us Billie because my head of department – James, you remember him? – is taking up a post at Cambridge after Christmas and wants me to join his team. It's quite prestigious and I'd like to do it. Obviously you'll still have another year and a half as an undergrad after that. Cambridge is not too far and hopefully you'll come across at weekends? I can also try to come to you now and then but I thought Cambridge might be fun. Drinking in the Eagle Tavern and all that. I know you love Rosalind Franklin.

Anyway, we can talk about that when we meet in Paris in three weeks. Hope I haven't dropped a bombshell but I thought you should know and James only told me last week. You are still up for Paris, aren't you? I'm really looking forward to seeing you again and having a few days walking around and exploring. Steak frites by the Seine and all that. That little B&B you booked in the Marais looks great.

Please write and let me know how it's going there. How is Lisa and how goes her stated attempt to find some hunk of a farmer's boy?

Grá mór,
Adam

4

The sun was rising in a cloudless sky above the hills towards Rapallo and down towards the Cinque Terre on what looked set to be another scorching day. In a few hours, the railway station at the top of the hill would be debouching Genovese day-trippers to enjoy one of the last Saturdays of the year suitable for a day on the beach and it would more resemble those times of early summer when he and Billie usually came. For now, though, Recoli was wistfully empty.

Having decided to obey Billie's voice of last night despite another interrupted sleep, Luke had set out on an early walk to the harbour, past the bookshop, past the basilica. Once through the archway, he stopped to take it all in once again. The harbour was the shape of an open envelope, one side providing a window to the sea, the other three offering commerce to both tourists and local fisherfolk. Bars, restaurants, ice cream parlours and a pizza takeaway sat alongside a ship's chandlery and a fishing goods emporium. There was also a cute shop selling luxury items such as leather bookmarks and antique maps. She'd never been able to resist going in there every day just because she liked the rich smell and the feeling that she was touching quality. In here, she'd bought him a Moleskine notebook with the initial L on the front. *'For your jokes,'* she'd said. *'Should last you a lifetime.'* He'd been unable to stop himself laughing. She, he thought, should have been the comedy writer.

He decided, after hesitating about the wisdom of it, to go in. The smell brought back the piquant memory. He saw the leather bookmarks still on sale on a corner shelf. He picked one up with the initial B on it. It was expensive but worth every cent. The woman behind the counter smiled at him as she placed it in a small pink paper bag.

Gripping it tightly in his hand, he walked to the furthest point of the harbour, to the bar that they both liked. It was always quieter here as most tourists never made it this far, waylaid by flashier establishments earlier in their promenade. The two of them could sit outside and enjoy in peace an Aperol spritz, just the odd passer-by to distract from the tranquility and the generous hors d'oeuvres of grissini, cheese, prosciutto and olives. Sometimes it sufficed for the evening if they'd had a long lunch.

The bar was closed of course, but he chose not to sit on the bench nearby. Instead, he wanted to check out the little passenger ferry that ran from here and back to the coastal villages and towns to the east. It was a bracing, enjoyable twenty-minute journey to a tucked-away cove accessible only by boat – a trip worth making due to a delightful restaurant, *Da Antonia*, and the monastery of San Pietro offering cool refuge from the sun and peaceful space for contemplation. Billie also liked the candles the monks made. '*We'll light them at Christmas and it'll remind us of a special summer past and the next one to come*,' she'd said. He saw that the ferry was running for another fortnight, and wondered if he had the stomach for making the trip alone, particularly given what happened on what had proved to be their final meal there. Even with the progress he had made, it might just be one act of bravery and grief tourism too much.

'Good morning,' came a voice behind him.

He turned around to see the red-headed woman in her pink velour tracksuit. Not forgetting the pink trainers. She smiled at him. Taken aback, he said nothing, neither offered a smile in response.

'Are you thinking of taking the boat trip?' she asked.

Aware how rude his lack of reaction seemed, in true British fashion he did not wish to compound his surliness by failing to reply. His surprise that someone other than a representative of the hotel's staff was speaking to him with more than a greeting made him falter, however.

'I'm not sure,' he mumbled.

He could see now, close up rather than a dining room away, that she was a woman of striking looks, not far from his age, possibly a few years younger. Her eyes were hazel, the edges of her mouth pointing north, as if used to smiling.

'They tell me it's an enjoyable and manageable trip and there's a very good restaurant near the monastery,' she said.

'All that is true,' Luke replied.

'You've been before?'

'I have. Several times.'

'I'll take that as a recommendation. Thank you.'

Luke nodded.

'My name is Ann Bradley, by the way,' she said.

'Luke Jessop,' he replied.

'Well, Mr Jessop. I hope you have a good day.'

'Thank you, Miss, Mrs...'

'Ms.'

'Ms Bradley.'

Luke watched her stride off back towards the hotel and noted her gazing at a device on her wrist as she did so. The demands of her step counter were clearly pressing.

As he took a seat in an empty shelter usually reserved for those waiting to board the ferry, he could not help but wonder about Ann Bradley. Why she was here, in Recoli? It was a remarkable and memorable place to those who knew it, but one off the beaten tourist track for foreign visitors. It took some finding, both in real life and online. People searching the internet for holiday destinations usually found what they were looking for long before they got to this small town, people except those like Billie who always delved deeper for the right B&B or hotel. And while the Miramare was a wonderful hotel, others in resorts with more diversions matched and even surpassed it. Why also was Ann Bradley here alone, what was her backstory? As soon as he caught himself wondering, he stopped. He should have no interest in this woman. He shook the thought from his head and began making his way back to the hotel.

In his room, he lay on the bed staring up at the ceiling fan once again and dredged up the memory of his last ferry trip to the cove that he had taken with Billie just over two and a half years ago. She liked variety in her life but loved the predictability of their holiday week and so it was always the same, always a highlight of their time here. This time, though, the cancer was debilitating her more and more, having progressed to her liver. It had been a monumental effort travelling here, especially through airports. Nothing could be done quickly. Everything was in slow motion. As was his memory now.

She was wearing that yellow dress with orange piping and the pattern of blue sailboats. She looked very 1960s chic in it, very French or Italian film, though it hung a little on her more wiry frame now. Her face was sallow, her hair wispy. They had booked a lunch at midday at the restaurant – the only time they could get in – so popular was it that June, but had left it late to catch the 11.30am ferry. And the next one wouldn't be for another hour. It was normally only five minutes' walk from the hotel to the ferry's mooring but in her condition now it would be ten at least and they had left at 11.20am. He looked at his watch and she chided him for worrying and said they would make it in time. Such reassurance did not stop him fretting.

He made to hold her arm as she laboured through the hotel reception and down the alley that opened on to the *lungomare* but she insisted that she could do this on her own. He so wanted her to be right. When they reached the arch that marked the separation of promenade and harbour, he checked his watch to see that it was 11.27am and she was breathing heavily. There was still about 100 metres to go.

'You go,' she said, almost shooing him on with her right hand. 'You get the tickets. You can ask them to wait a minute for me.'

He was reluctant to leave her, especially when seeing her struggle so, but he knew she would be angry if they missed the boat and their lunch reservation. He dashed on and reached the ticket kiosk in a minute. Thankfully there was no queue, with everyone who was making the trip now aboard. He paid swiftly for two returns and ran to the ferry where a young man was pulling in the gangplank from jetty to boat.

'*Un minute, per favore,*' Luke said, his own breath now short. The boatman shrugged his shoulders, said something about *tiempo* and continued tugging at the gangplank.

'*Mia moglie ha il cancro,*' Luke blurted out.

He had learned that phrase before coming on this holiday. He sensed it might be needed. The c word was to be used only sparingly, only desperately. Now was one of those times. The boatman looked at him for a moment and stopped what he was doing. Luke turned his head to see Billie now some twenty-five metres away and pointed to her. The man nodded his head, said 'OK' and Luke went to get her, guiding her on to the boat via the gangplank as she clung to the railings either side. He knew she would not be able to climb up the ladder to the top deck as they always had on their previous three visits and so they settled for a seat on the lower deck at the stern.

Billie was disappointed not to be up top where the view was better but as the boat left the harbour and swung out into the open sea just five minutes later, her face lit up again at the prospect of the journey. By now she had her breath back and they had the lower deck to themselves. He took her hand and, before the boat rolled in the sea's chop at its full throttle, led her to the bow. There she could feel the wind on her face, and smell the salt in the air, and she laughed like a child, loving the sensations. A tear had come to his eye – brushed quickly away lest she read anything worrying in it – blamed on the wind and its saltiness.

Though only a short trip, it was twenty minutes that sated the senses. As they headed east, their gaze was fixed to their left. 'Is that port or starboard? I never know,' she said. 'Port,' he replied, a veteran of cryptic crossword clues. There, the majestic coastline, with its forested hills cascading into the rocks and beaches and sea, opened up a panorama they always recalled when Billie suggested every January that they might book again. He had readily agreed every time.

Fortunately, the restaurant was in a corner of the cove and just 100 flat metres from the ferry's mooring. They would not be going up the steep stone steps, carved into the hillside, to the monastery this year. Now there was no rush to make their lunch booking and so they took their time along the path that curved around the cove to the restaurant. Signora Aguello welcomed them and allocated them a table on the decking with a fine view of the beach, with people taking to the water as the heat of the day came to its peak.

They ordered the same dish every year, the *lasagnette al pesto*, the dish on which the *Da Antonia* had established its reputation and for which people made special trips. The sheets of pasta were like silk handkerchiefs, the sauce so distinctive because the basil leaves were fresh and grown locally with a particular flavour found nowhere else. Billie had once asked for the recipe and Signora Aguello had generously confided its contents but it hadn't tasted the same at home and Billie had cooked it only once, not wishing to sully magical memories.

Billie sat sipping her white wine, the local Pigato, and luxuriating in her sense of wellness deceptively induced by the fine cuisine, the shade from the early afternoon sun and the idyllic location. Luke modestly moved to the back of the beach and changed into the bathing shorts he had brought with him, and swam in the warm, whistle-clean water of the cove. He front-crawled some 40 metres out from the shore, having had the foresight to bring his goggles, and watched curious fish dart hither and thither as he startled them. After a few minutes he stopped and turned to look back towards the restaurant terrace. He waved and Billie waved back. He loved that she had been watching him and responded immediately. He was in the moment, and happy in it. It may have been the last time he was.

But then suddenly there was no more waving. He could see her no longer. And he could just make out Signora Aguello standing at the table, with a circle of other people having gathered around her. He swam back to the shore as fast as he could and sped up to the restaurant. When he reached the terrace, dripping wet, he could see Billie was prone on the decking. A waiter was clearing up a small flow of vomit from her mouth. Concerned diners, some horrified, were trying not to stare.

'Billie,' Luke shouted. 'My God, what happened?'

'She has fainted,' said Signora Aguello. 'We have called for a doctor.'

Luke, shaking, kissed Billie's forehead. 'It's all right, my darling. I'm here.'

Billie, awake, stirred and began to try and lift herself.

'God, that limoncello's a bit bloody strong,' she said.

Luke laughed with relief, beginning to cry at the same time.

'I think maybe that was my fault' said Signora Aguello. 'I offered it to her with my compliments while she waited for you.'

Luke helped Billie to her feet and she sat back at the table.

'I am sorry,' she said to Signora Aguello. 'Was I sick on the floor?'

'Do not worry,' came the reply. 'All is fresh now. We have seen this before.'

'Really? I always thought the food here was better than that,' said Billie. To Luke's relief, Signora Aguello had understood the joke.

Billie then looked around at the disconcerted diners at other tables. 'It's OK,' she said. 'It wasn't the food. You'll all be fine.'

There was an uneasy, subdued laughter around them. God, Luke thought, she could be magnificent.

A doctor arrived in thirty minutes and checked Billie over, offering her a couple of paracetamol. She had been fine once rehydrated and rested but it had been a foretaste of what was to come over the next few months.

Now, as he lay on the hotel bed, the memory of her on the floor intruded brutally on the vision of her waving to him as he swam. A tear came to his eye, and a smile to his face. They frequently accompanied each other these days, twins but of differing temperaments. He had been wallowing in his memories, but why not? Especially when they represented a past that was so much better than the present or the prospect of the future. Besides, this was what he had come here for; to prompt reminiscence through these familiar surroundings, to linger over the rose-tinted, to experience then discard the dark, as that article on pilgrimage had insisted was possible. *Come on*, he told himself, *you should expect by now not to know what might result and why.* He had come to understand that he was the prisoner of some process over which he had no control.

He looked at his watch and saw that just fifteen minutes remained until breakfast ended. He heard her voice urging him to get a wiggle on and so he hurried downstairs, hungry from his earlier walk, and dived into the buffet. The scrambled eggs were sloppy remainders now, the speck greasy from sitting in its stainless steel tray, but he cared little. The fruit was fresh and the coffee energising. He remembered a conversation with Billie about the toast in Europe and how it never tasted the same as at home. As well as French and Italians baked baguettes and pane, they could not, he felt, emulate the British plain white sliced loaf. *'And why would they want to?'* Billie had asked. He had drifted back into his own thoughts with little to observe today in the dining room. There was just the British couple ignoring each other; no Scandinavians nor Germans. And no Ann and salt-and-pepper man.

The reason for that, he discovered as he walked back through the lobby to bring from his room all that was needed for a morning by the pool, was that they were heading out for the day. She was wearing a yellow dress. The man's right hand was in the small of her back again, his left carrying a picnic basket. She didn't see Luke. In fact, neither of them seemed to be aware of anything going on around them, so absorbed with each other were they. As they left the hotel, Luke edged across the lobby to get a view of them walking through the car park. When they reached a red Alfa Romeo sports car, the man opened the passenger door for Ann, who got in elegantly. From the driver's seat, the man pressed a button to open the roof. Showily, he revved the engine as if on the Monza grid and soon the car was speeding through the square and up the hill to the main road out of the town.

Luke saw Massimo at the reception desk and took the chance to speak to him.

'The painting by the breakfast room...' he said.

'Yes, Mr Jessop.'

'Do you know the artist and whether he might sell prints of it?'

'Of course. His name is Adriano Montelli and he lives in Milan. We commissioned it from him. Let me get you his email address. You can ask him yourself.'

Massimo returned with the address written on a piece of paper and Luke thanked him, before heading outdoors for a morning by the pool. Once on his sunbed, he sought to relax, to read a book, to start a crossword. But he was restless and irritable. He noticed the serene Scandinavians and the wealthy Germans on the other side of the pool. He picked up his computer tablet and scrolled listlessly through the newspaper apps before reminding himself that he was here to escape all that. He was here to honour memories, and Billie's memory. He ordered some coffee and mineral water almost for something to do. He sipped both without enthusiasm when they arrived. He was angry with himself and his indecision, thinking once more that he should go home but feeling that it would be a cop-out if he did.

Then, to his embarrassment if not quite shame, he could not resist googling Ann Bradley. He felt a frisson of nervousness as he typed the letters. There were plenty of women of that name on social media but none had a picture in their profile resembling her. He tried again with Anne, even Anna, in case he had misheard, then scrolled through timelines to see if he could perhaps identify her but he knew nothing about her – where she came from or what she did for a living – so could not narrow it down. He called up Google images and there was a photo that resembled her, accompanying her profile on a business site. He dared not click on it. He feared that the site registered the interest and internet profile of any browser who did and he did not want his curiosity to be discovered.

Sighing, he laid the tablet to one side, put his sunglasses on, and lay back on the sunbed to sunbathe for a while before it got too hot. He was annoyed with himself for allowing this woman to infiltrate his thoughts. He recalled a conversation with Billie that came a few days into one of their holidays here after they had been monitoring their fellow guests and gossiping about their comings and goings.

'Strange,' Luke had said, 'how small incidents and episodes assume ridiculous significance when you're away from home on holiday because there's nothing better to do.'

'Just as I like it,' Billie had said. 'It's because your world becomes smaller.'

He'd smiled at the time, but now he knew what a smaller world really meant, one with no one else in it on a daily basis, and he sighed again.

He closed his eyes to try and relax for as long as he could bear the heat and until the regular internal debate about whether he should stay or go repeated itself. Within a few minutes, however, he felt the warmth of the sun on his face replaced by a cool shadow. He opened his eyes and sat up, startled.

'The very helpful woman at reception said I'd find you here,' said Adam Byrne.

5

Luke removed his sunglasses, partly in surprise, partly to get a clearer look at the figure standing over him. As he rose, Byrne offered him a hand. At first Luke was stunned into inaction but then he did what he thought any Englishman should do and shook it.

'This is a bit of a surprise,' said Luke. 'A lot of a surprise actually.'

'To me too,' said Byrne.

They stood in silence for a moment. Luke took in the panorama of the swimming pool and the sea beyond, the beach below them filling up, before looking back at Byrne.

'Well, thank you for coming, Adam,' he said. 'Can I call you Adam?'

'For sure, yes.'

'Look,' said Luke. 'I was going to get an early lunch on the terrace. Would you like to join me?'

'Thank you. I'd enjoy that.'

They walked side by side, neither looking at the other. Luke was wondering what to ask. Or, rather, where to start with his questions. The bereaved all, always, have questions for the dead – unanswerable by them, Luke knew, of course he did, but perhaps answerable by others who had known them. He had rehearsed asking Adam Byrne his questions so many times. Two days ago he'd been prepared for a meeting, was the instigator of its timing. It was one reason why he'd been so calm flying out here. And, despite some natural and manageable nerves and doubt that grew when he reached the village, he'd been in control of the situation there and then. Now he was on the back foot. It was Byrne who had determined where and when the meeting was occurring. Luke's mind, like his heart, was racing with possibilities and pitfalls.

The waiter seated them at a table under a large canopy with a view of the beach and town. Luke was relieved that the terrace was not busy, thanks to many people being away on day trips or still lounging by the pool. He did not want their conversation overheard, wanted privacy for any sharing of intimate details there might be. Instinctively, they took chairs adjacent to each other rather than opposite.

'It'd be a shame to turn one's back to this view, for sure,' said Adam.

'Indeed,' Luke replied, knowing that this way they could avoid eye contact, or at least establish it only when both wanted. Luke was comfortable with that. It meant that they might feel able to speak more freely rather than shrivel to pregnant silence under the other's gaze.

Luke picked up the menu. 'What do you like the look of, then? The seafood linguine is outstanding here.'

'Yes, it is,' said Adam. Noticing Luke's surprise, he added: 'Christine and I come here occasionally, for weekends, just a Saturday-night stay usually. Mostly out of high season. It's well known in the region.'

'Ah yes. Right. Of course it would be.'

Adam cut short the pause that followed.

'I'm intrigued that you want to speak to me, I have to say. It was all such a long time ago, and Billie and I had nothing to do with Billie and you. Different eras, different stories.'

Luke nodded. 'What made you change your mind?'

Adam shuffled in his seat. 'I'm sorry about the other day. I was uncomfortable with you being on my territory, I guess.

More specifically, I didn't want Christine mixed up in any talk of Billie. She was round at a friend's and I knew she'd be home at any time. I couldn't speak. She would have hated it.'

'How come?'

'Billie made her life hell in our early days. Finding out her home number and ringing her. Calling her all sorts of names. There was a pretty serious episode…'

Adam paused for a moment and shot a glance at Luke, who was now looking intently at him.

'She never wanted anything to do with Billie again,' he continued. 'Or to hear anything about her. I never mentioned her name again.'

'So what did you tell Christine about who I was?'

'I told her exactly who you were. And that I didn't want to speak to you. That it was a part of my life that was long gone. The same as I told you.'

'And what have you told her about today and coming to see me?'

'I haven't. I'm at the football with Pippo.'

'I beg your pardon?'

'Pippo. I think you met him. The bar owner in the square? You'll know him as Filippo. He's a Sampdoria fan.'

'I'm sorry, I know nothing about football.'

'Sampdoria are a Genoa team. They're playing Milan this afternoon. Big game. I go with Pippo sometimes. He pays someone to mind the bar for a few hours. He drove me here and is going on to the game. He'll pick me up later.'

'I see. And you're OK with lying to your wife?'

The words came out more aggressively than Luke had intended. He didn't want to spook Adam into curtailing this encounter. Adam contemplated the question for a moment.

'Lying. It's such an emotive, black-and-white word, isn't it? And black and white doesn't always work when it comes to relationships, does it? There are subtleties and nuances. Issues and episodes that don't fit into truth or lie. I have things I'd like to say to you and to hear from you. And I suspect you're the same. Christine is not a part of this and would not want to be. I'm respecting that whilst doing what I believe is the best for all three of us. Four perhaps.'

Luke pondered Adam's words carefully before formulating his response. Clearly he hadn't upset the man by challenging him and so pressed on.

'That all sounds like self-justification to me,' he said. 'You're telling me there should be secrets in a marriage?'

'Whether there should be, I don't know,' Adam replied. 'But there probably are in all marriages. We all have things personal to us, from previous lives maybe, that might be better left not spoken about or heard tell of.'

'That,' said Luke, 'is what used to worry me a lot. Still does to some extent. It's just that I feel I ought to know. I want to know all that I missed. Everything about Billie.'

'As much as anyone is ever likely to know everything about Billie,' Adam replied. 'Or about anyone, let's be honest.'

'I'm jealous of you,' said Luke.

'How so?'

'You got to be with her in her twenties. I would have liked that.'

'Maybe you wouldn't. If you had, maybe it wouldn't have lasted.'

'What does that mean?'

'Well, when you met Billie, perhaps she'd learned from some volatile times with me and was ready to settle and commit. With you. Perhaps I'm jealous of you for being the one who benefited from my mistakes. Then again, I've been happy with Christine.'

Adam smiled and the waiter appeared. They both ordered the seafood linguine. Neither wanted wine in the heat of the day and so they shared a large bottle of sparkling mineral water.

'Where do you want to start?' Adam asked once the waiter had left.

'OK, right. Well, I think I know about how you and Billie met, and the early years of your relationship.' Luke went on to précis what Billie had told him. After growing up and school in Wolverhampton, she'd gone to Birmingham University to study film and television. She'd met Adam – eight years older than her, and a part of a research programme into cancer treatment – during fresher's week.

'I promise you I wasn't some predator,' Adam said.

'Oh, no, I wasn't suggesting...'

'She was with a friend in the bar, as was I, and we just got chatting. She clearly liked older men. I mean, what age are you?'

'Sixty. I was five years older than her,' Luke replied.

'Exactly. She told me that she was bored with boys of her own age at school. Immature and only interested in one thing. Her father had died of cancer when she was sixteen, and she was fascinated by my work. I'd done medicine at Trinity in Dublin and got this very good research position at Birmingham."

'Looking for a father figure? A healer?'

'Bit simplistic, I think, but an element of truth. But then, at that time of life, an eight-year age gap is not huge. There was of course a physical attraction as well.'

Luke wasn't sure he wanted to hear about that, or at least not yet, and steered the conversation away. 'She was somewhat vulnerable by the sound of it.'

'Perhaps. But I promise you, our relationship was something of a slow burner. I had no intention of taking advantage of the situation. What else do you know?'

Luke said he knew facts but not detail. That they had been together for almost ten years in all but only lived together for the last five. That Billie had gone abroad for her summers whilst at university, and Adam had moved to another research programme at Cambridge but the relationship had continued, mainly at weekends and in vacations. That after university she'd managed to get a job as a producer on a TV news show in Southampton and that, after a couple of years of the two of them getting fed up with the distance between them, he'd landed a job as head of a research programme at the university there. And that they'd then bought a house together in the New Forest.

'That's pretty much the bare bones of what I know,' added Luke. 'I know that Billie wanted to take up a job in London but you didn't want to go with her and that you then met Christine and wanted to sell up and move on. I only know from letters that I found that there was a wrangle over the house.'

'Yes. Those letters…' said Adam.

'To be honest, I only read the last one, which was on top of the pile, and the first one on the bottom,' said Luke. 'And there were some diaries of hers. I checked entries around those two letters. The first one was when she was in Switzerland one summer and she thought you'd written a rather needy letter, wondering what she was up to.'

'I felt sure she did meet someone that summer,' Adam replied.

'There was something in the diary entry about her meeting somebody, yes.'

'As I thought, then.'

Luke was concerned that he had stirred some hurt feelings in Adam. He wanted both to be honest and to reassure him. 'Her friend Lisa had told her she was foolish to commit to a boyfriend in her first year, and her head was apparently turned by some boy her own age she met there. But she also said that she found you brilliant and caring.'

'Well, thank you for that,' Adam replied. 'That summer was a long time ago and bothers me no longer. I'm not going to dwell on it.'

'Her diary entry after receiving the final letter those years later was an angry one,' added Luke. 'About how she hated being dumped, and that she was not going to make your and Christine's life easy when it came to selling the house.'

'Well, she made good on that resolution.'

'I felt bad reading about the ending and the beginning of your relationship, and the diary entries. Like a voyeur. But maybe you can understand… I couldn't stop myself delving into them. Guilty curiosity. I stopped after those two letters because I wasn't sure I wanted to know the ins and outs, especially if they were intimate. I put them back in the box.'

'So why do you want to talk to me?'

'Back when I first found the letters a few months after she died, I got this queasy feeling, which was why I locked them away again. I was raw and vulnerable in my grief at the time and couldn't take any more anxiety. Now I feel I have some equilibrium back in my life and think I can cope with things I might hear. And I wanted to hear, rather than read them. To hear from somebody who also loved her. To compare notes.'

'I see. Sort of.'

'In the first year, I visited lots of her school and university friends and cousins and aunts. Her mother died ten years ago. You may not know that. I enjoyed finding out things about her when she was young. Hearing their memories. Now I feel that way with you. I still love talking about her.'

'Did her uni friends say much about me?'

'All of them said you were a nice guy, placid, and that Billie could be… well, difficult.'

Adam chuckled. 'Yes,' he said enigmatically. 'To be honest, I think she found me difficult as well, in a different way. For placid, read staid. And let's just say that I didn't express my feelings as readily as she did. She probably just got bored with me.'

'Then why did she get so upset about the relationship ending?'

'A bit of pride, I think. She didn't like the idea of me taking up with someone else. Herself as the one being left. I reckon if anyone was going to do the dumping, she would have preferred it to be her.'

'There was something about a final straw in your last letter to her…'

'I suppose it could be seen as amusing now I look back on it,' he said. 'At the time it was bloody scary. She came bursting into my research lab one afternoon, demanding to know where this Christine woman was. I'd mentioned her a few times and said how nice she was and Billie had got jealous. She'd imagined things were going on between us. She ran between labs until she found her and started shouting at her, hurling all sorts of names and abuse at her. Security had to be called.'

'Wow,' said Luke. 'Billie and I had our moments but nothing quite like that.'

'I think she felt ashamed of herself afterwards. She apologised and we didn't mention it again for the next few weeks, but I was never going to get over what happened.'

'So *were* you and Christine…?'

'That's the funny thing. We liked each other but no, not at that time. This episode was probably the thing that threw us together. After that, we gravitated towards each other, and a month or so later I knew I wanted to be with Christine and to get a long way away from Billie. For her, I think it was a salutary experience. You two got together, what, three years later?'

'Sounds about right,' said Luke.

The food arrived and they began to eat in silence, lapsing into small talk for a break from the growing intensity of the conversation – about the view, the food, and how Luke and Billie had come here four years in a row and loved this coastline. Luke said that Billie had liked how the waiters took orders with pen and paper still, as example of the human touch of the place. But it was mere prelude to what Luke really wanted to know.

'Do you feel able to fill in any gaps for me?' he asked, wiping his lips with an immaculately laundered napkin.

'You seem to know the basic facts pretty well,' said Adam. He paused before adding: 'Billie was a hard person to love, to be honest.'

'Meaning?'

'You have to remember she was eighteen when I met her. It was her first real relationship. I think there were times when she agreed with that Lisa friend of hers that she shouldn't have committed to me so early on at university. What you tell me about that diary entry you found after I wrote to her in Switzerland confirms it.'

'Your letter back then talked about meeting up in Paris. Did you?'

'Yes, we did. I did have my concerns and suspicions. She was a bit off with me. I sensed something had happened in Switzerland but she steered clear of the subject. Now you tell me about her fling. It doesn't matter now. We were young. She was very young. I always thought she kept secrets.'

'I thought so too.'

The waiter arrived, not only to collect their empty plates, unwittingly breaking a moment of tension, and they ordered a panna cotta each. Luke noticed that the British couple had taken a table on the other side of the terrace. He hoped they'd strike up a conversation so that they would not be overhearing his own with Adam, but the early indications were not promising. Luke lowered his voice.

'So I know how it started and how it ended, but how was it in between?'

'Where do you start? I mean, we were together, if only loosely at times, for almost ten years,' said Adam. 'You know about our jobs and times apart. That's what the letters were. No internet, no mobile phones. We'd speak on the phone maybe twice a week, on payphones during student days. I remember those grim winter Sunday evenings when speaking to her would be a highlight of my week if she hadn't come to stay that weekend.'

'A good friend of Billie's told me she thought you two would be together for ever.'

'I thought that too once we'd survived the separations and got the house in the New Forest. But strangely, the closer we were physically, the further apart we became emotionally. She was ambitious; I wasn't. At least, not for a job in London. My ambitions were all about developing cancer drugs.'

'She was a very good TV producer,' said Luke.

'Yes. So I believe. Local news was never going to keep her. She liked the idea of drama and comedy. Got shifts in London and would travel up during the week, come back at weekends. Wanted us to move there permanently. The two of you met in comedy, right?'

'Yes. I was writing for a TV sketch show. She joined as an assistant producer. Look, I get how you became different people with different wants and needs but why did it get so acrimonious, do you think?'

'Asking for a friend?' Adam said, raising a smile from Luke. 'The first two years after we moved into the house were good,' he continued. 'Well, goodish. Billie was always feisty.'

'She hated that word,' said Luke. 'And with some reason. Said it was only women who were described as feisty. Men were called passionate.'

'Fair point. Back in the 1980s and early 90s, there wasn't the same awareness or acceptance of women's roles and rights, though. Strong, gutsy women like Billie were just seen as high-maintenance and hard work. I guess I'd been brought up to see women that way too. My mother was very easy-going.'

'So Billie's, what, sparkiness would have been attractive to you because it was something new?'

'Yes, I suppose so.'

'And me,' said Luke. 'But I guess for different reasons. My mother had a temper, and I could have my moments too, I confess. That was probably why I married my first wife, who was a calm person. She finally tired of me trying to write jokes and then getting frustrated and angry if and when I didn't or couldn't. She found someone else more in tune with her.'

'You and Billie must have had some ding-dongs, then.'

'Yes, we did.' Luke laughed at the cameos of arguments that suddenly rushed through his mind. Scenes of Billie shouting, of him shouting back. 'I was terrified when we first argued after the first few months of dating and being nice to each other in case the other bolted. I'd never had rows like that. And it could be over something trivial, as I thought. Like me being late for something. Or going out to something I'd forgotten to tell her about. She'd even lock the doors from the inside to try and stop me from leaving. Disproportionate reactions. Then, as we opened up, I realised it was to do with her background, her fear of being left on her own, as she was now and then when her parents went away for the weekend. That happened back then to thirteen-year-olds more, I guess, but I think it was traumatic for her and gave her a fear of abandonment. I came to realise all she wanted really was a hug. If I could get over my own fear of her temper and cross the room and hold out my arms, usually she'd respond with tears and a hug and the meltdown would end.'

He looked expectantly at Adam, who looked back at him.

'I recognise all that,' said Adam. 'But I don't think she had an understanding of what was going on with her then. I certainly didn't. And it wasn't something I wanted to explore, to be honest. I don't think at that time of her life, or mine, we were ready to. Now everybody wants to investigate these things, don't they? Wants to know what drives their relationships. What their issues are.'

The panna cotta arrived and they ate again in silence. The British couple were still saying nothing to each other, just sitting, staring out to sea, waiting for their meals to arrive.

'Men found Billie very sexy,' said Adam. 'That was another problem, particularly in the last couple of years of our relationship. She was flirty. Liked the company of men. And she always enjoyed sex. Well, until she didn't with me.'

Luke shifted uneasily in his chair. He looked across at the Brits, whose noses were now buried in paperbacks. At least they were not overtly eavesdropping.

'You know,' Luke said, lowering his voice. 'When she was alive, I never worried about her being unfaithful. I knew that we loved each other. We were just getting on with our lives, me writing, her producing shows. Even when she travelled abroad on shoots, it never bothered me.'

'But?'

'But since she died, I've worried a lot that she had affairs. As you say, she was flirty. Vivaciously attractive to men, I'd say. To be honest, the thought, the vision, of her having sex with another man, has haunted me.'

He looked across at Adam, who returned the eye contact. Thankfully, there appeared no judgement in it and Luke looked away again and continued.

'Grief, you know. It finds chinks in your emotional armour. It's invasive, worms its way in. The sadness brings echoes of all the pain you've ever felt in your life. And from a young age.'

'Which was, in your case?'

'My mother had an affair. I remember my father being devastated. But he loved her so much, and was so frightened of life alone without her that when the man threw her over, refusing to leave his own wife, my father accepted her back. I was twelve years old and knew it was all happening. It traumatised me, to be honest. And it was never spoken of again after she came back. I never trusted my mother in anything after that. I thought she loved me. Loved my dad. But she slept with another man. And it coloured my relationships with women.'

'In what way?'

'I was always worried that they would let me down and leave me. Was always walking on eggshells around them. My fear manifested itself in anger. It's what men do, isn't it? We're good at anger. As deflection from our vulnerability. It duly happened with my first wife. Became a self-fulfilling prophecy and she left me for another man. But then I met Billie and we fell for each other. She seemed so devoted to me. I felt settled, confident in her. Now I wonder.'

'Do you feel jealous when I talk about sex with her?'

'In my gut, yes. In my head, no, not really. Because it was long before I met her. It's really just what might have happened in the years of our marriage. All my past insecurities have come back to haunt me. I mean did. In the first year after her death it was obsessively unnerving. Now I'm less exercised by it, though still fascinated by her and her life. Which is why I came to see you. Even in death and her absence, I feel defined by her. She still has a huge power over me.'

Adam nodded as they each sought to absorb the significance, to both of them, of what had just been said.

'Billie had a power, all right. There was certainly something all-consuming about her,' Adam said. 'Even when we became distant in the last couple of years of our relationship and slept in different rooms, she was hard to get out of your head. She'd be home late from the studio some nights. I sensed she had affairs, usually brief.'

'That's the sort of thing that makes me worry,' said Luke.

'I guess that was why I was attracted to Christine. She was the same age as me. Very different from Billie. Consistent. More like my mother. Who appears to be very different from yours.' They both smiled before Adam continued. 'Billie stayed with friends in London at first when she started getting the freelance shifts, then rented a room somewhere and stopped coming home at weekends. I rang her up and said I wanted us to sell the house. She insisted on getting three valuations, and then holding out for the highest one.'

'Well, I can understand that if she was going to have to find somewhere in London.'

'Yes, but when I told her that Christine had been coming to the house since the incident at the university and we were a couple now, she began to get very aggressive. She started ringing Christine and shouting down the phone at her. In the end, we both decided that we wanted a fresh start abroad, and a pharmaceuticals company in Genoa were hiring so we both applied and got positions with them.'

'I'm guessing Billie dug her heels in.'

'You guess correctly. She kept refusing to sell the house when we got offers for it. Said they weren't high enough, even when they were just a few thousand short. In the end, we went anyway without the house being sold. It became a stand-off; who needed the money most and who blinked first. It went on for six months. Then Billie got fed up with a bedsit and wanted to buy a flat instead and relented. In the end, it went for less than the first offer we'd had. That was the market then. It was a stressful time.'

'I suppose that was why you were glad to cut all ties. Billie once told me she was sad that you and she had never spoken again after you broke up.'

There was a silence.

'When did she say that?' Adam asked.

'Oh, a fair while back. Five years before she died, maybe.'

Adam checked his watch. 'Look,' he said. 'There's about

forty-five minutes until Pippo gets back to pick me up. Can we go for a walk? Maybe get some coffee on the *lungomare*?'

'Sure,' said Luke. He summoned a waiter and signed for the bill, declining Adam's offer to split it. Luke saw they were being watched by the British couple, who smiled at him, and the two of them left and made their way down towards a café overlooking the beach. Luke ordered an Americano, Adam a double espresso.

'Beautiful here,' said Adam. Luke nodded and they sat in silence again, taking in the late-season sights of the colourful parasols of those who could afford slots on the private beaches, and the towels laid on the shingle for those who couldn't.

Adam took a sip of his espresso before breaking the silence.

'Billie and I did speak again. In fact, she came to see me.'

'What?' Luke said, stunned.

'It was after her breast cancer diagnosis and the first chemo and she was back working. She got my email address through someone I'd stayed in touch with from our Birmingham days. Said she was going to be working in Monaco for a week and could she come and see me.'

'I remember that. She was production manager on a drama.'

'Well, she took a day off and got the train to Genoa. We had some lunch in a nice little restaurant at the port.'

'What did she want?'

'Fish,' said Adam. 'The sea bass, I think.'

'No,' said Luke, annoyed that everybody seemed to be a comedian these days except him. 'What did she want to see you about?'

'She wanted to apologise.'

'For what?'

'For making mine and Christine's life so difficult. She'd been in a bad space, she said, worried about the future and starting again. She felt guilty about things she'd said and done.'

'I see.'

'I think the cancer had focused her mind. She wanted to make peace.'

'Were you OK with that?'

'Yes. I forgave her.'

'Didn't you want Christine there to hear the apology?'

'Christine would never have wanted to see Billie. She wouldn't even have entertained her. She was so upset back in the day. Anyway, I didn't know what she was going to say so I knew it would have to be on my own.'

Luke sat silenced, trying to imagine the scene: unbeknown to him, Billie having lunch with a man she had once loved. He realised he felt no jealousy, however, and was relieved about that as a sign of his progress. He was pleased also to feel a gratitude that the woman he loved had been able to do something that had assuaged her guilt and brought her some peace.

'Did you speak about anything else?' Luke asked.

'We talked about our lives, how things had worked out for the best and we had both found partners that we loved and were good for us.'

Luke thanked him for saying that.

'She also said she really liked the coast along here and that she'd like to take a holiday here with you. I recommended a town called Recoli. This town. And a hotel called the Miramare.'

Luke shook his head and smiled. 'I guess I owe you then that we had some of our best times together here. This became a very special place for us, which is why I've come back. To access some memories, some highlights. Try to get some sort of perspective.'

Adam spread his arms wide and said that he was happy to have been of assistance.

'Why couldn't she tell me that she had been to see you?' Luke wondered.

'Possibly because she understood where your insecurity and jealousy came from. She knew your family history and the baggage you carried from your first marriage and thought it would cause a big argument between you. Maybe even a rift.'

'I suppose so,' said Luke. 'She was probably right.'

'That's why it's not always best to tell your partner everything, I reckon. In fact, it might be selfish to do so.'

Adam leant across the table and put his hand on Luke's arm.

'Listen. I'm absolutely certain that she really loved you and you alone, you know.'

Slowly a tear made its way from Luke's eye down the side of his cheek. He took out a handkerchief and dabbed it. The waiter arrived with the bill and Adam picked it up.

'Hey, don't cry,' said Adam. 'It's not much. Only eight Euros. And I'll get it.'

Luke laughed loudly through his tears, almost as a relief from his tension. The trip was picking up, even if he was a little unsettled just now.

They walked back to the hotel to find Pippo standing in the car park and leaning on his Fiat. He smiled when he saw Adam approach.

'*Due a zero,* Adam! *Due a zero!*'

'*Magnifico,*' Adam replied. '*Forza Samp.*'

Pippo held out a hand to Luke, who shook it.

'Good to see you again Luke Jessop. I am glad you and Adam got to talk.'

Luke asked him if he had been OK with driving Adam here, of keeping the meeting between Billie and Adam from Christine, who was also his friend.

'Yes,' Pippo said. 'We are all – how do you say it – men of the world, and we know what we need to do without hurting our partners.'

'Crikey. Is there some kind of club for you men out here?' Luke said. 'Come to think of it, your anthem is called *Fratelli d'Italia*, isn't it?'

'Careful,' said Adam. 'You're in danger of snapping out of the humourless grieving widower persona.'

Luke smiled. He wondered what Adam would say to Christine about the match, but Adam said not to worry, that Pippo would be giving him an in-depth report on the drive home.

'Listen,' said Luke. 'It's not really any of my business, but that first year after Billie died I went pretty crazy due to my own worries and not addressing them with her before she passed, not talking about things that came to bother me. None of us is going to get out of this alive, and one of you and Christine is going to go first and the other will be left behind, so I'm just saying maybe think about telling her about meeting Billie? And meeting with me?'

Adam thought about it for a moment but said nothing, opening the passenger door of the Fiat. He was about to take his seat when Luke said, 'Oh, wait. Stay here a moment,' and dashed into the hotel. Luke reappeared a few minutes later with the box of letters. He'd removed the diaries as Billie would have hated Adam to have seen those, let alone owned them. Even more than she would have hated Luke seeing them. They were hers, and hers alone, Luke had decided anyway, unlike the letters.

'I think this belongs to you,' he said to Adam, who smiled and took it from him.

'I'll let Pippo keep that for me until I can smuggle it into a safe place,' said Adam.

Luke shook Adam's hand and waved the two of them goodbye as they drove off. He was just about to turn back into the hotel when a red Alfa Romeo pulled into the car park. No sooner had the car stopped than the passenger door opened and out stepped Ann Bradley hastily, slamming the door behind her. She strode intently towards the hotel, past Luke, contempt on her face. Behind her, the man had got out of the driver's seat and was shouting, ' Ann! ANN!' much to her indifference.

Luke couldn't help but chuckle. You wait three days for a laugh, he thought, and two come along at once.

6

Luke gazed out to sea from his low perch on a wall on the *lungomare* in the warm light of a new day. He was in something of a trance as he reflected on exactly what had happened yesterday and what he planned to do with his last full day here before flying home tomorrow. It was 7.15am, around forty-five minutes past the waking hour that his muscle memory now accepted.

He had been unable to face another solo dinner in one of the hotel's restaurants last night. Instead, he'd walked into the town, taking in the streets on the upper levels to mull over his conversation with Adam and recall the times when he and Billie would buy snacks and drinks for their room from the small supermarket, fruit from the little shop near the railway station. By the harbour, he'd bought himself a pizza and eaten it on the beach, watching the lights of Genoa rise and twinkle in the twilight. Back in the room, he'd watched a TV show of football highlights fronted by a woman with gigantic blonde hair just to see Sampdoria beat Milan 2-0 and feel connected again to Adam and thus a young Billie.

As Saturday had become Sunday and once again he found himself staring up at the ceiling fan, he had replayed over and over in his mind the encounter with Adam. There was a part of him, now that he thought about it more, that was angry Billie had been to see her first lover, had kept it from him. He had to admit, though, that he had kept secrets from her. When his first wife had been ill some eight years ago, he'd been to visit her in hospital. But then, she was the mother of his son; there was always going to be a bond between them. He hadn't said anything because, like Christine, Jane was resented by Billie and had once been on the receiving end of a tongue-lashing down the phone. What was that one about? Something to do with insisting they have Jude for a weekend when Jane was going away and Billie had tickets for a concert at the Festival Hall for the two of them. Luke had agreed to Jane's request, of course, because he enjoyed the time with the then teenage Jude, but he had hated being torn between the only two women he had ever loved, one peacefully but no longer, the other crazily but enduringly.

And so he hadn't told Billie about that hospital visit. Because Billie was… well, Billie. If you pressed her too much on anything, she would simply turn the conversation into conflict, deflect the escalation on to you, question where you'd been, why and what you thought you were doing. It was never a contest really. She would always win. Not just win. He would always end up feeling he had done something wrong. My God, she was good. He smiled at the memory. Once, it had filled him with fear; now, he would give anything to hear her questioning him. He had come to see it was about her own insecurities, not his shortcomings. He wished he'd understood that better then.

In the quiet of the early hours last night, he fancied he had heard her: *So what if I went to see Adam? I had unfinished business with him, OK? You're not going to deny that to a woman with cancer, are you? No, it would have been different with you going to see Jane if she was ill. What, she was only going to get well if you took her grapes and magazines?*

Of course he wouldn't have denied her the visit to Adam but then that too, he now saw, was about her own insecurities; that he might be angry with her and punish her, abandon her, as her parents had done. Sometimes he didn't dare walk across the room to hug her due to his own fear of rejection. Turbulent waters ran deep, and Billie did not want to risk her vulnerability being exposed again. As he'd read in one of those grief books immediately attractive in the aftermath of death, the more complicated the relationship, the deeper the regrets.

What he was certainly angry about was Adam's recommendation of this hotel. His gratitude expressed to Adam had been mere politeness, he had come to realise. He had needed little encouragement to admire Billie's taste and her eye, and had been especially fulsome in his thanks and praise to her for finding the Miramare. Now he felt almost deceived, as if Adam had at least a part share in what was their place. Billie, he recognised, was not alone in her insecurities about past relationships, however much he felt he had made progress, however much like an adult he had behaved with Adam.

Luke had tossed and turned for at least a couple of hours, trying not to check the time on his phone. It was just like the early days after she died. There were things he did not know about her, about their life together and apart, and it provoked a powerful anxiety in him. He admonished himself for his childishness, told himself to grow up. Then he remembered to be kinder to himself. That he was not being ridiculous. That he was still grieving. This was not linear, after all. It was not a gentle progression within a finite time frame towards acceptance of her death and his life without her. There were jagged rocks and here-be-demons caverns. Echoes of past fears, insecurities and jealousies stemming from his family of origin. *Be kind, be kind*, he repeated to himself. *Coming here to Italy was bound to reignite the embers of doused fires, of course it was.* He had known none of that in the first year, just fear upon fear, pain upon pain. Eventually, time and just putting one foot in front of the other, going backwards sometimes, had brought him at least to a point where he could mop the sweat of panic with some acceptance of both his situation and himself.

Such compassion, however much in the darkness of night he felt he did not deserve it, at least turned his mind from his ire at the rekindled verbal intimacy between his late wife and her ex-lover and towards something Adam had told him: '*Listen. I am certain that she really loved you, you know.*' He recalled the times she said it too. '*I do love you*' – that night twenty years ago when they had climbed into bed on their wedding night, she giggly with bubbly. '*I do love you*' – that time he'd taken her away to a five-star spa hotel for the weekend when she was low in the midst of the first chemo. '*I do love you*' – that morning, drowsy with the morphine, when he'd placed a cold flannel on her fevered forehead. Whispering it to himself almost as a mantra last night had finally brought the sleep his racing mind and aching body had craved.

Not that it helped past his customary waking hour, no matter how late sleep had finally accepted him. Mostly these days he woke without the knot of anxiety that the first year had brought and having had at least a few hours of unbroken sleep. Today, though, he was edgy anew. The trip had taken him from that routine bringing comfort and control. Typical of him, he thought, to focus on the disturbing things that Adam Byrne had said rather than on the most important line of all. He would be grateful to get back home tomorrow, to the comfort and control of his usual routine.

In such an agitated and weary state, Luke decided that on his final full day he could not face alone the boat trip to San Pietro and a lunch at *Da Antonia,* given the dark memory of Billie fainting. It was, he reflected, one thing to make a pilgrimage to a place where pleasant, shared memories could blossom, but quite another to revisit a traumatic episode that could propel him into yet another black hole. Instead, he worked out an itinerary in his head of a trip to a place where nothing to frighten him had occurred. He would set out early, too. Already the sun was promising another searing day.

Luke rose from the wall and walked back towards the hotel for breakfast. There had been no pink velour tracksuit and matching trainers to wish him '*buongiorno*' on his early walk this morning, he suddenly thought. She'd either gone home last night or was heading off this morning. No sign of her at breakfast either. He ate a hearty one, taking comfort in food. He also filled two bread rolls with cheese slices and tomato and took a banana and a bottle of water from the buffet, as Billie used to do for them when they were going on a day trip.

The bus journey from Recoli to Sta Margherita Ligure, just a few miles away through and over the hills, was spectacular. It wound through hamlets, where the doors of the bus would hiss open and widows in black would alight with their shopping bags, followed by young students with backpacks still a week or two away from college. The view on the descent into the town was to cry for as the bus curled its way down through residential streets lined with palms. When it reached its destination on the seafront, the memories arrived again in waves. Her voice echoed in his head. '*Let's walk along the beach. Do you mind if I go to that shop again? Shall we have a coffee in that shady place down that side street by the church?*'

He wanted to feel the fine sand of Sta Margherita between his toes, so he took off his canvas shoes and walked past wooden changing huts painted in stripes of blue, red and white. The beach and town were naturally quieter than on his previous day trips here during summer seasons with Billie, but still some leisured folk lingered, lured by the unusually hot weather. He had a vision of Billie taking off her shoes and them walking together here. From habit, he held out his hand to take hers before checking himself. He stopped, looked around and wondered if anyone had seen a movement that must have looked odd to an observer. He contemplated extending both arms as if to mime that he was stretching but then remembered, quite apart from the paucity of spectators, that he really wasn't that interesting and probably nobody had registered the moment.

Luke turned back into the town itself and towards the chic little womenswear shop where she had bought something every year. The cuts were Italian and fitted and suited her slender frame perfectly. She had bought those polka-dot trousers here, that figure-hugging brown dress. That yellow light summer coat that now hung on a hook in the entrance hall of the house as a reminder of her colourful presence – the presence of absence – whenever he came home.

Impulsively, he entered the shop and began to browse. There were no other customers, just a woman behind the counter folding a new delivery of sweaters that would not be sold in this day's heat but would be ready for the autumn season.

'Can I help you, sir?' she asked, used to the signs of Englishness. 'Are you looking for a gift for someone perhaps?'

'No. There is nobody,' he said, realising that he could not leave it at that. 'I wonder… do you remember an Englishwoman who used to come in here? Every year, for four years in fact. Until three years ago.'

'Billie, you mean?'

'Yes, you remember her?'

'Of course. She always bought one item, sometimes two, every year. I think now I recognise you. You came in here with her the first year, but sat outside mostly after that. She liked to take her time, I know. Yes, you are Billie's husband.'

'Luke,' he said. 'I'm so glad you remember her.'

'I am Gabriella. This is my shop. I am sorry for your loss.'

'You know?'

'Well, yes. Yes, I do. We became email friends. She would write to me a week or two before you came to see if we had some items that might suit her. I would send her some pictures.'

Here was something else Luke didn't know. It wasn't important, nor sinister, and nothing he would have needed to know, but suddenly again he felt there might be more things of which he was unaware and the feeling of queasiness – at once familiar and unnerving – insinuated itself into his stomach.

'When I didn't get an email one year and didn't see you both that summer, I had a feeling something might be wrong. She didn't look well that last time you came in. I tried the internet and entered her name and I saw something from a website for television people about her death. My sympathies, Luke.'

'Thank you. Life is a little better. I have come back, you know, just to remember.'

'It is a good thing to do. Thank you for coming into my shop. I liked Billie.'

Luke smiled, complimented Gabriella on her lovely shop and left, grateful for her comments and memories. He was struck again by how much of an effect Billie had on people while he felt he was just an appendage of hers in many ways. He considered once more that he was still defined by being her husband, her widower now. To be anything else, he still believed, would be to betray her and to lose the mantle of an identity he had slipped on to his shoulders, much like the cardigan of hers he would curl up in, weeping, in a foetal position on their bed in the months after her death.

He found the little coffee bar in the shady street and ordered a double espresso with a small bottle of *acgua frizzante*. He was annoyed, embarrassed, with himself for feeling miffed that he had been excluded from something. Why should Billie and Gabriella not exchange emails? Why should he have had to know about it? It didn't matter. He had many people he corresponded with that Billie wouldn't have known about. But, on top of yesterday's revelations, it just made him question whether he was excluded from other areas of her life. Had Adam been telling him the whole truth? Had the man just been trying to spare his feelings, tell him what he thought he wanted to hear? God, this was back to the first year of the ridiculous jealousy when madness was heaped upon sadness. When aloneness fuelled a mind's racing. Would he ever be over it, free?

Oh for God's sake grow up, Luke, he imagined her saying. *You have women friends, don't you? You go out for dinner, don't you?*

Actually, he hadn't. Didn't. He wouldn't really have dared to. And Billie expected different standards from others. She liked to amuse men and be amused by them, but heaven help him if he had behaved that way with women at a party within her earshot. The drive home would always feel a long one. He chided himself for being so unkind about her now. There had been times during their marriage, he had to admit, when he wondered why he stayed. But then, a friend he had confided in said that was pretty normal. Now, in her absence, he knew it was because of her singular magnificence. And the sheer eventfulness that she brought to his life. As he would say to that friend: 'I guess I've had many different relationships – with the same woman.'

Luke could take the internal dialogue no more and so paid his bill and made his way back to the seafront and the bus stop. He hesitated at the ticket booth, contemplating one more trip to Portofino. Something inside him was insisting that this would be the last opportunity so he should take it. The snaking ride clinging to the shoreline was full of breath-taking vistas at each turn. Out to sea, huge and luxurious private yachts were at anchor, between legs of their journeys along the coast, from Marseille to Rome. Billie had downloaded an app that would tell you to whom they belonged, enjoyed looking them up on her phone.

Portofino was still busy, if not as crammed as in high summer, with the cruise ships plying the grey-pound trade and the smaller ones docking here, unloading their curious ageing clientele wishing to touch the hem of celebrity the village had acquired in its Elizabeth Taylor and Richard Burton heyday. The place was much smaller than he remembered, the only area to walk really being a couple of streets dotted with the odd shop and then the harbourside parade of bars and restaurants.

He sauntered idly by them, thought about having an early lunch at one that looked pleasant enough, with outside tables in much-needed shade under a canopy. Then he studied the menu and remembered why he and Billie had not dined here before. Did it really matter any more that prices here were ten Euros more than in Recoli? He could afford it these days and, as he kept telling himself, he would not be coming back here again. But then he heard Billie's voice again: *I'm not paying that. Let's go.* He smiled and remembered the contents of his shoulder bag, which nostalgia now made seem preferable, and so he found a communal bench in the shadow of a tree on the other side of the harbour and ate his cheese and tomato rolls there, toasting her with his bottle of water.

An hour was enough – he preferred the homelier, less glitzy charms of Recoli – and so, with the sun now at its most oppressive, he decided to head back and perhaps have a swim and a nap. Having no especial fondness for Portofino, save for Billie once having walked its streets with him, he did not look back nor say a farewell. It was different at Sta Margherita, where he changed buses. He stood gazing out to sea as he waited for his connection then turned to look again towards the womenswear shop. Smiling to himself, he heard her again: *You big softie. But we did like it here, didn't we? Even if only for a few hours during our week.*

On the bus home, all the views were behind him and he had to turn his head now and then to enjoy them. The journey was never, he recalled, quite as beautiful going back.

*

Luke awoke from his nap with a start and looked at his watch. The sun was swiftly sinking over Genoa and he had about twenty minutes to perform his task. He had promised himself he would do it on his last evening, and would do it at sunset. Billie would have been dismissive of the sentimentality, he reckoned, but only superficially. Deep down, she would have approved of the gesture and been touched.

He scooped up his shoulder bag and walked briskly down to the church, finding a spot on the end of the promontory. The light was crepuscular now but there was still enough for him to see what he was doing, to light the lantern in her memory and send it down into the sea a metre below for it to drift out. He had bought it online, a pretty paper replica of a pink water lily with a tea light at its hub. He would send it into the Mediterranean at this spot they both loved and pay homage to his departed wife with a few well-chosen words that he had been rehearsing in his head to mark the occasion. That, at least, was the plan.

Luke clambered to a flat rock a foot or so above the water line and took the lantern from his bag along with a box of matches. He supposed he would light the tea light, bend down and give the lantern a gentle nudge on its spiritual journey out to sea. The short film he had been directing in his mind had not really taken account of the weather, however. A southerly breeze, though gentle, saw him go through half a dozen matches and he began to worry this was not going to work. He grew edgy. On the seventh strike, he managed to light the candle and cupped his right hand over the flame as he lowered himself to bended knee.

'Farewell my lovely,' he said as he prepared to set the lantern on to the water. But just then a breath of breeze suddenly sent the flame sideways towards the paper and it caught alight quickly. Luke yelped, his fingers burned, and dropped the flaming object into the water where it hissed and died. His elegant speech also went up in smoke. 'Bugger,' he said loudly and leaned forward hurriedly to dip his hot fingers into the soothing cold water.

Suddenly he heard a short but loud laugh behind him. He stood up and turned to see Ann Bradley standing there, her hand over her mouth, clearly embarrassed by her involuntary outburst.

'I'm so sorry,' she said. 'I couldn't help it.'

Luke looked at her aghast.

'Can I ask what exactly you're doing?' she said.

'No, you bloody can't,' he said 'Can I ask you what you're doing standing there?'

'I was out for a walk and I saw you. Thought I'd just say hello.'

Flustered, Luke could not immediately think of a reply. He just stood there bemused for a moment before shaking his fingers and wincing with pain.

'Were you trying to burn something? That's not very environmentally friendly.'

'What? Look it was biodegradable, OK. I made a point of buying one that was.'

'One what?'

'That's none of your business.'

'Have you singed your eyebrows? There's a bit of an odd smell...'

'What?' He checked with an index finger to find that he had. Ann's unwanted observation and the flurry of burnt hair fluttering before his eyes tipped him from snappy to snappier. 'Look, I'd really rather you moved on, if you wouldn't mind please. I was trying to do something rather important and I was hoping for some privacy.'

Ann looked hurt. 'Forgive me,' she said, before nodding and turning away. She walked briskly back in the direction of the hotel, not looking back as she went. Luke watched her go for a few moments.

'Bugger, bugger, bugger,' he said loudly enough for a startled couple passing by to stop and look disapprovingly at him. He stared down at the sea below but just a few small black pieces of paper floated, swaying in the swell of the water around the rocks.

'I am so sorry, my darling. I seem to have cocked that right up,' he said. He recalled something she said one Christmas morning after he had gifted her some lacy Rigby & Peller underwear that was more for him than her and seen the surprised look on her face: '*I suppose you expect me to say that it's the thought that counts, don't you? Well, it is. And the thought of you going into the shop all embarrassed and buying these for me has made my day. Thank you. You've even got the size right.*'

He smiled ruefully. He had done his best. It was indeed the thought that counted. And he was sure she would have laughed at the realism of the movie as it turned out rather than the schmaltzy one he had scripted. In fact, she would have laughed pretty much as Ann had done.

He didn't feel like dinner conspicuously alone again tonight, even though it was his last night and he had thought he would order the best thing on the menu. Instead, he went to the pizza shop and bought himself a couple of slices. As he sat eating it on a wall overlooking the beach, he began to feel uneasy, however. In his embarrassment, he had been unkind to Ann Bradley. She was only being friendly. Only saying hello. She wasn't to know that he was performing some kind of rite that was sacred only to him, a grand gesture that had gone awry. He too was now beginning to see how comical he and the whole scene must have looked. The second slice of pizza suddenly lost its appeal and he tossed it in a bin. There was something he needed to do.

When he reached the hotel bar, he noted the Scandinavians drinking an aperitif at a table in one corner, enjoying a convivial conversation by the look of it, while the English couple, watching him intently, sat in another, ignoring each other. Luke then spotted Ann, sitting at the bar with her back towards him and sharing a bottle of Dom Pérignon with the two Germans. He was relieved that she was there and he could speak to her.

'Um, excuse me,' he said.

Ann turned around.

'Oh, it's you,' she said. 'Hello again.'

Luke looked a little embarrassed as the German couple stared at him. He smiled at them and they took the hint, picked up their flutes of Champagne and settled at a table out of earshot.

'Look, about earlier...' said Luke.

'You've still got some charred eyebrow hair on the end of your nose,' Ann replied.

'Really?' He went to wipe the end of his nose.

'No, I'm joking.' She smiled. Luke was too flustered to reciprocate.

'I'm sorry about my reaction. You startled me, and I was doing something rather private.'

'That doesn't sound good.'

'What?' A penny dropped. 'No. Oh, God no. I was actually lighting a lantern in my late wife's memory at a place we both loved.'

'Oh dear. I am so sorry,' Ann replied, mortified. 'Had I known...'

'Of course. There was no way you could have known.'

Awkwardness enclosed them like a straitjacket.

'Can I buy you a drink?' Ann said. 'By way of an apology?'

Luke considered it for a moment.

'No, honestly. Thank you anyway. I think I want to be on my own for a while.'

'Of course, I understand.'

Luke turned to go.

'What about tomorrow?' Ann said. 'I feel I'd like to apologise properly. Can I buy you lunch?'

'No, seriously. It's fine. Apology accepted. I hope you accept mine?'

'Of course.' Ann pressed on. 'Listen, I've booked a table for lunch at that restaurant in the cove at San Pietro. The one I was recommended. The one you said was very good. The *Da Antonia*? I'm sure they could set another place on my table. Please join me.'

Luke answered without even thinking: 'I'm afraid I'm going home tomorrow. I have a flight late morning.'

'Ah, that's a shame. Could you perhaps stay an extra day?'

There was a silence. Luke pondered the possibilities of the moment in a few flashing thoughts but quickly rejected them.

'I don't really think that's going to be possible,' he said.

'Understood,' said Ann. 'But if things change, or you do change your mind, I'll be getting the 11.30am ferry.'

Luke smiled at her, turned to go and this time she said nothing to stop him.

Back in his room, he thought some more about yesterday and his conversation with Adam, realising he was less angry, less concerned now about the renewed acquaintance between Billie and her ex. She had been different when she'd come back from that shoot in Monaco, he remembered now that he replayed the time in his mind. Affectionate towards him. He remembered feeling warm towards her too, having missed her. He thought about today and his goodbye trip to old haunts, a gratitude rising in him that he had come to know this place so well, loved it so much. Above all, had loved his time here with her so much.

He also thought about this evening and Ann Bradley. He was intrigued by what had happened between her and the Italian yesterday. He'd certainly like to know more about that, about what went on and how it ended. He smiled at the memory of Ann striding off and ignoring salt-and-pepper man's protestations. He also thought about how beautiful San Pietro was and the remarkable food at *Da Antonia,* a place he was being offered the opportunity to revisit in company rather than enduring the discomfort of going back alone. It was somewhere he may not have wanted to return but that – maybe, who knows – might prove valuable if he did. After all, that pilgrimage article had talked about risking pain to achieve a greater peace.

He took his laptop from his holdall, found the bookmarked website and checked seat availability, this time not for an earlier flight but one from Genoa to London for the day after tomorrow.

7

Luke was early, by fifteen minutes. Unable to endure again what he experienced the last time he made this excursion, he had given himself a ridiculous amount of time to get here.

It was another hot morning, sunny, his phone telling him that the temperature was already thirty-one degrees, and he sat at the ferry mooring watching the remnants of the summer season creak into movement. With the weather set so fair, there would be still be good business to be done, but this was a Monday; the majority of the parasols on the beach remained down, and the bars were only just beginning to stir. The fellow travellers waiting to board the boat numbered around twenty rather than the hundred or so who might have been here in high summer. He felt agitated, though not beset with anxiety exclusively. There was an excitement coursing through him too. He told himself not to be such a ludicrous schoolboy and felt a flush come to his cheeks.

At 11.20am the boat opened for boarding and all alighted, save for him. He looked at his watch. Perhaps, like him, she didn't want to go alone. He should have told her earlier that he would be coming. Then again, she'd said just to turn up, hadn't she? He hadn't considered that she might duck out. Perhaps, like him though, she'd had a change of mind. She only wanted to go if accompanied by a man, he thought unkindly. He reproached himself for that but was more annoyed with himself for going through this rigmarole, for having kept his room on and put his flight back by twenty-four hours. For wasting fifteen Euros on a return boat ticket. There's no fool like an old fool, he reminded himself. He looked at his watch. It was 11.29. The boatman looked at him standing on the dock.

'Signor?' he enquired.

Luke realised he couldn't face the memory of San Pietro on his own. He shrugged his shoulders and turned to walk away.

Suddenly he caught sight of a running figure. She was wearing sunglasses, holding on to a wide-brimmed orange sunhat and sporting a long, floaty light-blue dress, a tote bag over her shoulder. She was about 100 metres away. He turned back to the boatman.

'*Un minute per favore*,' he said to the boatman, who was beginning to withdraw the gangplank. Luke pointed to the running figure, and the boatman smiled and nodded, no longer under pressure from the captain of a cargo of people all excitedly wanting to be on their way. The mood was relaxed today.

Ann bought her ticket hurriedly and dashed to the boat, where she saw Luke waiting for her.

'Gosh. Good morning. I didn't think you'd come,' she said. 'Thank you.'

'I think,' Luke replied, 'we ought to get on the boat and exchange pleasantries then.'

'Of course,' Ann said, taking a step onto the gangplank, aided by the outstretched hand of the boatman, who escorted her onto the deck. Luke followed, knowing he was an afterthought for them in that moment. He was unconcerned. He wanted a moment to stare at the stern of the boat, then take his eyes to the bow, and remember that last time. When Ann turned around, having thanked the eager boatman for his help, she pointed to the top deck and Luke followed her up the wooden steps.

She took a seat towards the front, holding her hat in the breeze, and looked excited. He sat down beside her as the boat's engines revved and it reversed from its mooring before heading towards the harbour entrance.

'Did you hold the boat for me? If so, thank you,' she said.

'My pleasure,' said Luke, doffing his panama.

'I forgot my hat and had to go back,' she said. 'Can't do without that on a day like today. So glad I caught this. I would have missed my lunch reservation if I hadn't.'

Luke smiled at her.

'I only decided definitely to come half an hour ago,' she went on. 'To be honest, I was having second thoughts. I mean, I'm used to doing things alone, but the temptation of a day by the pool almost overwhelmed me. Then I thought, *that's just lazy, Ann. You're here till Friday. You can always do that tomorrow.* She paused. 'I'm gabbling, aren't I?'

Luke smiled again.

'Anyway, it's lovely to have company. So glad you changed your plans and came. What made you decide?'

'I'm interested to know why you were angry with that Italian chap the other day.'

Ann looked confused at first, then disappointed.

'Oh, him. Less said about him the better. Let's just enjoy this trip, shall we?'

'As you wish,' said Luke.

Once through the mouth of the harbour, the boat turned east. Ann got up abruptly, startling Luke. With plenty of seats available, she moved to the other side of the boat and sat down. Luke wondered if he had said or done something to upset her, but she called across the aisle. 'It's better on the port side. We can follow the coastline more clearly. We'll sit on the starboard side coming back. Please, join me.'

Luke hesitated before rising and sitting next to her. 'You know that port is left and starboard is right?' he asked.

'Yes. "Port" has the same number of letters as "left". That's how I remember. It helps with cryptic crosswords.'

Luke nodded. They settled down to savour the short journey. Ann was clearly energised, her face lighting up as she pointed out the Miramare. Luke had seen it all before but was moved by seeing it again now. He stared at her as she held on to her hat, admiring her red hair cascading on to her shoulders like burning lava. He could not help a tear descending from his eye beneath the cover of his sunglasses at a memory of Billie being similarly excited. Ann turned from the view of Recoli just in time to see him bringing a handkerchief from his pocket to dab his moist cheek.

'Is all well?' she enquired.

'Yes. Just the salt and the wind in my eyes. Makes them water.'

'Isn't this marvellous?' she said, turning back to admire the rugged, rocky coastline topped by trees that had replaced the boundary of the town. The elegant, tall flats in all their glorious colours of terracotta, pink and yellow were receding into the distance.

'Yes,' he said, being reminded. 'It is.'

Twenty minutes later, the boat pulled into the jetty at the beach of San Pietro. Ann's lunch reservation was for 1pm, she said. She had planned to walk up to the monastery and take a look around, work up an appetite. Was that all right with him?

Indeed it was, he replied. And, beyond any politeness, it was. Having been concerned about making this trip again and reliving the painful episode, worried about feeling an overwhelming sadness, he was suddenly glad to be here. Perhaps he could bring to mind more the previous three years, when visiting this place and eating the food was the highlight of their week. Yes, being with someone could make that possible. Returning to the monastery, which they had been unable to do that last time, would bring back those best of times.

'Excellent,' said Ann and she set off up the steep steps.

Luke was more used to this place being crowded and plenty of people going in either direction, providing ample opportunities to stop and rest as the lines concertinaed. Today there were no obstructions, no need to pause. It seemed not to trouble Ann, who ascended the steps comfortably and consistently. In the first year after Billie died, Luke had put on a stone due to the transitory comforts of sugar and though he had lost half of it by mostly resisting the siren lure of chocolate, he still felt overweight. Halfway to the summit, breathless, he just had to pause. He remembered that there were sixty-eight steps and he found was counting every one of them.

At first, Ann did not notice but then she turned to see him panting in the midday sun, a mad dog of an Englishman. She retraced her last dozen or so steps.

'Everything all right?'

'It will be,' he struggled to say, embarrassed as he clung on to a railing. 'I apologise,' he added. 'I'm a little out of shape. What with... You know. What with everything.'

'Please don't worry. Our bodies do start rebelling at our age, don't they?' she offered generously.

He was reassured by her understanding and by her sympathetic relating to him, if only in age rather than condition. She was svelte and clearly fitter than him – and a few years younger. His breath settled and they set off again, this time reaching the top of the hill and the monastery without any further interruptions.

'Let's sit on that bench over there,' she said.

'No, honestly I'm fine now,' he said.

'Actually, I'd like to rest. And to enjoy this view.'

'Oh, sorry. Of course.' It had been a while since he'd had to consider someone else's needs.

They sat looking out to sea, tankers and cruise ships lining the horizon. Luke had been doing his best not to think of Billie, but a pair of large-lensed sunglasses on a female face, a rush to board a ferry and a discussion about port and starboard meant that it was inevitable that he was going to fail. Expecting himself not to call Billie to mind was unrealistic, especially since the whole purpose of this pilgrimage had been to do just that, to picture her again. Today was a good day thus far, a day when he could appreciate that and be a little easy on, rather than angry with, himself.

'Magnificent,' said Ann.

'Indeed,' said Luke.

'How come you know this place so well?'

'I came here every summer for four years with my late wife. We always came to San Pietro once during our stay and ate at *Da Antonia*. She was one of those rare people who still bought reliable guide books rather than relying on the vagaries of the internet and she found this place. We loved it here.'

Ann reached down into her tote bag and produced a guide book.

'One like this?' she asked.

'Yes, one exactly like that,' he said and smiled.

A moment taking in the view passed before Ann broke the silence.

'Would you like to tell me about her?'

'Not really, if you don't mind. I'd rather hear about the man you seemed very angry with on Saturday.'

'Carlo? Oh, if I must. That's easily dealt with.'

'Carlo. Hmm. Interesting.'

There was a pause. Luke turned his head to look at her. She became aware of him staring and looked back at him. She started giggling, prompting Luke to smile.

'Seeing you stride away from his car did make for rather a comical scene,' said Luke.

'It didn't feel funny at the time,' Ann replied with a laugh. 'But I guess looking back it was.'

'So come on, spill.'

'Nothing much to spill. He was on his own at the hotel; so was I. He introduced himself to me, and I got on reasonably well with him, even if he was a bit full of himself. He asked me if I'd like to join him for a picnic, which he got the hotel to supply. I thought, *why not*? I mean, it's company for those of us on our own. I was getting a little fed up with seeing all these couples dotted about the hotel. Some of them even took pity on me, I think, and invited me to join them for drinks now and then. Funny, isn't it, how they assume we need rescuing?'

Luke issued a lame smile. He wondered if he too was just company for a lonely woman. He began to reconsider the wisdom of being here. He had resisted coming to San Pietro over the weekend not just because of the fainting episode and his own panicked reaction that might rekindle old anxieties but also because of the potentially overwhelming beauty of this place where they had been at the apex of their togetherness during weeks in Recoli. If he was honest with himself, he had sometimes feared coming away with her as they could be fiery with each other. At home, he could escape the house and drive off in his car if a serious argument developed. There was no hiding place here, and no escape. His fears had quickly been proved groundless, however, and as soon as Billie boarded the plane, she relaxed into her natural attractiveness and vivacity, while he felt accordingly relieved. Yes, he had shied away from returning to this spot as he feared the reappearance of both the idyll and the horror, he realised. Now he was hearing about some dalliance between a woman he barely knew and a random man whom he did not. He cared little for their possibly tawdry tale just now, and began to feel miffed that he might have been earmarked as a replacement Carlo. He was brought back from his thoughts by her continuing her story.

'So he drives down to Rapallo in his rather sweet little sports car and we have a wander round and some rather nice coffee and then he heads towards the Cinque Terre. I think we are going to have our picnic somewhere on the cliffs around there, but before that can happen, he diverts the car to some quiet woods he says he knows. I suspect he'd been there several times before. Anyway, he lays a blanket in a clearing in the shade and unpacks the food and wine. I must say that it was all rather lovely. Until I begin to realise that I'm on the dessert menu and he moves close to me, puts an arm around my shoulder, takes my hand, kisses the back of it and tries to move his way up my arm towards... Well, towards who knows where because I didn't wait to find out. I soon put an end to all that. I was surprised how red his cheek was afterwards.'

'You won't have that issue with me,' said Luke, seeking to reassure her. 'I'm not likely to be risking a slap.' Ann looked a tad embarrassed.

'What? Oh no. I wasn't suggesting you might...'

'It's OK,' said Luke. 'No offence taken. Please carry on.'

'Well, I asked him to drive me back to the hotel pretty smartish, which he did without argument, to be fair. He even apologised, saying that I should forgive him because seduction was Italy's national sport.'

Luke just had to laugh. Ann joined in.

'Yes, that was pretty funny, I have to admit. When I got back I googled him. Turns out he's a dentist in Milan with a wife and two grown-up kids. Grandchildren as well. I spoke to one of the waitresses at the hotel who is fortunately rather indiscreet and she said that he comes here alone for weekends every six weeks or so and leaves alone. In between, though, she said, "he is not always alone, Signora." Dodged a bullet there, I reckon. All I can say is, his wife must believe there's a lot of weekend dental conferences on around the place. Unless she has her own reasons for wanting to get rid of him for weekends.'

She looked across at Luke, who had been watching her intently as she told the story while she had been looking out into the distance at the sea.

'What?' she said, with a mix of embarrassment and self-deprecation showing on her face that Luke enjoyed.

'No. I'm just amused. Thank you for telling me.'

They sat in silence for a few moments longer before Ann rose to her feet sharply.

'Right, shall we go into the monastery?'

'Why not?' said Luke, following her lead.

As they crossed the threshold to the imposing white-stoned building, Ann took off her sunhat and rested her sunglasses on the top of her head. Billie used to do that, he remembered, before telling himself that they probably weren't the only two women in the world to do so. He put his own sunglasses in the top pocket of his shirt and took off his hat.

The building provided a welcome respite from the now intense heat of the day, the flagstones cold and its darkness offering enveloping balm, like so many religious Mediterranean buildings. They ambled through, taking in giant paintings of holy scenes hung from the walls, and Luke recognised the stations of the cross. Ann stopped to sit in a front pew, absorbing the ambience and the sights, particularly the huge image of Christ on the cross behind an altar draped with silky purple cloth. Luke noticed her bow her head and kept walking, seeing a black metal rail of tea light candles behind the altar in the apse, the octagonal dome of which they had been able to see from the boat as a landmark. A box of matches lay to one side of the rail and he struck one to light a candle, carefully placing in it one of the holders before obeying the sign urging him to deposit a Euro in a slot in the wall. Memories clearly came at a price, if a reasonable one. At least he hadn't burned himself this time.

Luke stood there in reverential silence for a moment before sensing Ann alongside him. He turned to see her and she smiled before moving away towards the exit and the gift shop. He joined her there as she browsed books about the history of the place, the aromatic and alcoholic drink concocted by the Benedictine monks, and the scented candles. She bought a couple of the latter, and he recalled Billie doing that on their last visit, saying that they would be nice at Christmas. They remained untouched, unlit in a kitchen cupboard. He would definitely get them out this year, he resolved.

Back out into the light, there was a pleasant cloistered walkway, its arches offering shaded views of the sea, across to the steps down to the cove and restaurant.

'Time for lunch, I think,' said Ann.

Luke nodded in response. He had been moved by his walk through the abbey and did not want any real conversation just now. He was hoping Ann felt the same, and as they made their way in silence through the cloisters, it seemed that she did. He appreciated her sensitivity.

She led the way onto the decking of the restaurant, where Luke stood in silence for a moment until Ann turned to him: 'Anything the matter?'

'No, no. I'll be fine,' he said as they were greeted by a stooped woman in her seventies, clad in black. Ann mentioned her reservation in the name of Bradley and, turning to Luke and extending an arm, wondered if they would mind setting an extra place.

'Signor Luke?' said the woman, surprise in her voice and eyes. Luke smiled; the woman did not.

'Signora Aguello,' Luke replied. 'How are you?'

Her tone was not entirely convincing when she told him he was welcome back at her restaurant and that it was good to see him. There was a suspicion in her eyes. He was a trifle bemused but had little time to dwell on it as she showed them to a table under the trailing vines on the terrace. The shade was welcome, with a soothing breeze coming off the sea some ten metres away.

'Obviously you've made an impression,' said Ann after the brief exchange of words between Luke and the older woman..

'Probably less me,' he replied, wondering why Signora Aguello had been cool with him. Had she been unhappy, rather than sympathetic as she showed at the time, when Billie fainted? Clearly she remembered.

'What's good here?' Ann asked, perusing the menu. Luke told her that everything was excellent but that the *lasagnette al pesto* was special, that a well-known London restaurateur had visited here once and put the dish on his own menu but it never quite captured the flavours, due to the importance of the local basil. He told her too that the sea bass was always fresh and caught in these waters, probably this morning.

'Sold,' she said and laid the menu back on the table. 'Shall we have a bottle of nice white?'

'I don't usually drink at lunchtimes.'

'Oh go on,' she replied. 'What have you got to do? I doubt you'll be called on to pilot the ferry back.'

He smiled and agreed. 'The Pigato is good.'

'Doesn't sound it.'

'Trust me, it's lovely. A yellowish colour, dry and fruity.'

'Sold again, Luke Jessop. It's nice to be out for the day with a connoisseur.'

Before he could bask too long in the expansion of his ego, Signora Aguello arrived to take their order. 'Good choices, as I would expect of you,' she said but there was no warmth in her words.

'So, tell me about yourself,' said Ann as they waited for their wine.

'I'd rather hear about you,' he replied.

'Gosh. That's unusual. A man who prefers to listen rather than talk about himself.'

The wine arrived and he gestured for Ann to try it, just as he had always deferred to Billie that way. The Pigato met with Ann's approval and she complimented him on his choice.

'Well,' she continued. 'I'm fifty...' She put her hand over her mouth and coughed.

'Sorry, I didn't catch that.'

'You weren't supposed to,' she replied. 'And I have a dog, a Labrador named Holly.'

'Is there a Mr Bradley?'

'Like it. No fishing. Straight to it.'

'No honestly, I didn't mean...'

Ann ignored him. 'Bradley is my own name and I always kept it. I was married but he turned into a cliché. Met a younger version. I've been divorced for five years now. Best thing about it was that we had a daughter, Edie. She's twenty-seven.'

'I like that name. And your life now?'

'You do like the nuts and bolts, don't you? I live in Putney. You know London?'

'Yes. I know Putney. I live in north London.'

'Ah, right. Well, I worked as an English teacher for many years, in various schools in south London and Surrey. Sixth form. A Dickens of a job, I always used to say.'

Luke smiled.

'Now I'm semi-retired,' she continued. 'I just do after-school extra tuition a few days a week to get kids through exams. Work from home. I have a nice life. Read a lot. Walk Holly on the Heath.'

'I'm envious,' said Luke. 'How did you find Recoli, by the way? I mean, there are more popular places along this coast.'

'I trawled the guide book. Didn't look as glam or busy or expensive as some of the other places. Seemed more... well, down to earth. Like me. Decided I deserved a decent hotel at this time of my life.'

Signora Aguello arrived with the *lasagnette* and both purred their way through the food. It was, Ann ventured, one of the most delicious dishes she had ever tasted. Luke was pleased; Billie had so loved it too. Often in the depths of winter, and through the coldness of chemo, she would remind them both that sunnier days would come again and they would be here, at *Da Antonia*, eating perfect pasta. And then she would remind him when they actually were in this position, that she had reminded him during the winter and they would laugh. Except that they hadn't had that conversation for three winters now. Ann could see Luke lost in his thoughts.

'Penny for them…' she said.

'What? Oh, just thinking how much I love this place.'

'Yes, it is very special.'

Signora Aguello arrived to collect the empty plates and Ann complimented her on the dish. She smiled and thanked her. Ann asked her where the restrooms were and was given directions.

'No Signora Billie this year?' Signora Aguello asked when Ann was out of earshot, seemingly a subtext in her voice.

'Billie died almost three years ago,' he replied. The woman looked crestfallen and ceased scooping up the used crockery. She clasped her hands to her chest.

'Ah, Signor Luke. I am so sorry. I wondered why we hadn't seen you both for some time.'

Luke responded with a weak smile.

'I knew she had the *cancro*, and we had that terrible moment with her the last time you came, but I didn't realise she was near the end. My – what is your word? – condolences.'

'Thank you. I wanted to come back. To a place that had made us happy. Though I did have second thoughts and it hasn't been easy.'

'Ah, then I thank you. If you were happy here, then that makes me very happy. I liked Signora Billie so. And now you have a new wife?'

She had not noticed that Ann had returned and was stood at her shoulder, though Luke had. Ann smiled.

'Oh no,' Luke replied. 'Ms Bradley, Ann, and I just met at the hotel. We were both on our own so decided to have lunch together and...'

'I'd stop digging if I were you,' said Ann, retaking her seat.

'Of course,' said Signora Aguello, trying to flick a smile that only Luke could see. 'I will make sure chef cooks only our very best two sea bass for you today.'

She departed with the empty plates amid an awkward silence.

'Tell me about you now, Signor Luke,' said Ann. 'Fair's fair.'

He paused, looked around the decking area, at people busy chattering and eating, easy with themselves and each other. He had felt that with Billie. Suddenly the prospect of self-disclosure provoked an uneasiness in him again about being here. He hated it resurfacing every thirty minutes or so.

'Clearly I lost my wife,' he said. 'Other than that, not much to tell. I'm sixty, if you want to know that.'

'Did you have a celebration to mark that?'

'No. Not really. My son, Jude, took me out for dinner.'

'How long were you married?'

'Well, it took us four years to tie the knot after we met, so eighteen years. My first marriage broke up, and I met Billie through work.'

'Great name, Billie. Was she a Wilhelmina? Unusual.'

'No. Her father liked jazz and blues. She was named after Billie Holiday.'

'Ah, very nice.'

'I was writing for a TV show she was producing when we met.'

'You're a writer?'

'Comedy script writer. Though I know what you're thinking: he doesn't look or sound like one.'

'Semi-busted,' she said.

'To be honest, I haven't written anything funny since she died. In fact, I haven't written anything.'

'Did you have your son with Billie?'

'No. I think she might have made a good mother but it never happened. She enjoyed her career. She could have done both, I'm sure, but we never really committed to it. I had Jude by my first marriage. He's twenty-nine now. They got on pretty well.'

'And you live where?'

'Chalk Farm, just north of Camden Town. After Billie died, I did think of moving to the coast as I grew up by the sea in Hampshire and missed it. But there are so many memories of her in the house that I don't think I could sell it. And her grave is in the cemetery at Highgate. Can't be too far from that. I have been thinking of getting a little flat in Brighton for the odd weekend. Hove actually.'

'Careful. You almost told a joke there.'

'A lame one. An oft-told one.'

'I like it there,' Ann said. 'I have the odd girls' day out there with Edie.'

'Many people do,' said Luke, his rusty social skills with the opposite sex bringing the conversation to an uneasy halt.

Thankfully for them both, Signora Aguello arrived with the sea bass, fussing over them now and insisting it was the finest along the whole Ligurian coast.

'*Buon appetito,*' she said, any scowl Luke thought he had previously discerned now a distant memory, instead a smile that told of sympathy and encouragement lighting up her face.

If the fish was not the finest on the Ligurian coast, then somebody between the French border and Tuscany was enjoying quite some lunch. Ann and Luke savoured every mouthful of tender fish, bronzed and buttered sautéed potatoes, and succulent tomatoes. Ann thanked him for seconding the recommendation that the hotel had given her. And for accompanying her. He graciously accepted her thanks with a nod of acknowledgement and they ordered sorbet and coffee.

'Do you know,' she said. 'I feel like a swim. The water looks so inviting. I've brought my costume and a towel and I think I could rent one of those changing huts over there. Why don't you join me?'

'I didn't bring a costume,' he said. Deliberately so, he didn't add.

'Do you mind if I do?'

'Of course not. I'll just sit here and have another coffee.'

'Don't pay the bill. We'll go halves. OK?'

'Sure.'

He watched her depart with her tote bag, eagerness in her gait. She emerged from the changing hut some 40 metres away in a bright-red costume to match her hair and stepped gingerly over the pebbles to the clear water of the cove. He couldn't help but recall his own last swim here, feeling the cool freshness of the water on his skin. He recalled above all Billie watching and waving at him.

He watched Ann swim her easy breaststroke for ten minutes or so and felt relieved not to have brought his swimming shorts, given his current shape and condition that was probably not as noticeable to anyone else as much as himself. Any Monday now he was planning a new regimen of exercising more and eating less.

Ann waved at him. As he waved back, he was hit by a surge of melancholy, a guilt at realising suddenly that he was enjoying himself. He cursed the crashing intrusion. Enjoyment did not seem permissible. Not when Billie couldn't experience it.

When Ann returned to the table, she was invigorated, her cheeks now matching her damp hair.

'That was wonderful,' she said.

Luke nodded. 'Looked fun,' he replied.

Across the cove, the 4pm ferry pulled in some ten minutes ahead of its return to Recoli. It was the last of the day so they knew they must hurry. They paid the bill, leaving a large tip. Signora Aguello said she hoped she would see them both again. Luke did not reply, doffing his hat instead and thanking her as Ann shot him a glance.

Pleasantly tired and well fed and watered, they walked the short distance around the cove to catch the boat. Threatening clouds had suddenly appeared in the sky out to sea, and were heading towards land, as the wind grew stronger and the sky darker. The temperature began to drop markedly as they boarded the ferry and took their seats on the top deck in the open air, this time on the starboard side.

'Dark clouds,' said Luke, pointing to the horizon.

'Bring waters,' said Ann.

'Sorry?'

'Dark clouds bring waters,' she replied. 'It's a line from *The Pilgrim's Progress*. You know, by John Bunyan? It's saying how soothing the rain can be after oppressive heat.'

8

By the time the ferry reached Recoli, the rain was lashing, causing bulbously beautiful ripples on the surface of the normally flat harbour water. On the choppy journey back, they'd managed to stay dry by taking shelter on the lower deck, along with the dozen or so other passengers, at least one of whom was sick over the side. When it was time to disembark and the boatman extended the gangplank onto the dock, no-one was looking forward to the open air and a soaking.

'What about that little bar over there?' said Ann. 'We could make a dash for it and have a drink until the storm passes?'

Adam followed the line of her index finger to the bar at the mouth of the harbour, the one he and Billie used to like best. He could see the appeal of her suggestion but he had his reservations.

'There's a couple nearer,' Luke replied.

'Yes, but that one looks the nicest. And it's only an extra twenty-five metres or so. Come on.'

Before he could reply, Ann had begun running towards the bar, along the jetty and the harbourside path while holding on to her hat. He had little option then but to follow. Thirty seconds later they both came to a dripping halt under a canopy, rainwater cascading from either side of it. Their hats had kept their hair dry but they still stood with water running down their faces and their clothes damp, both trying to get their breath back, the sprint having tested their lungs. It was still warm, though the searing heat had been washed away.

'How about we take a table here?' said Ann. 'Seems dry under the canopy and it's fun to watch the rain come down when you're out of it, isn't it?'

Luke was grateful to have come through the expedition to San Pietro better than he had expected. Signora Aguello had been kind and Ann had been good company. The reassuring food had helped too, and the memory of Billie on the floor of the restaurant and his own distressed reaction back then had not overwhelmed him. He had misgivings about extending his good fortune, but he told himself he had come this far. Surely he could sit here, as he had with Billie, for another half-hour? The dark inside of the empty bar, in which he had never sat before, did not look inviting and he agreed with Ann. Being in the dry while rain lashed down around you was a satisfying sensation.

'OK,' he said and they took a seat. Soon a young waitress was with them to take their order. He and Billie had always enjoyed an early-evening aperitif with the generous antipasto they provided here. But it was still late afternoon, an hour at least away from alcohol time. Anyway, they'd shared a bottle of wine with lunch.

'I think I might have a cup of tea. Do you serve tea?' Luke asked the woman. Before she could answer, Ann had chimed in.

'Sod that. I'm having a glass of wine,' she said. 'Go on. Live a little.'

Luke went along with it. *In for a penny*, he thought.

'Good,' Ann replied. 'I liked that Pigato. Let's have another bottle of that.'

The waitress nodded and said she would also bring them towels. They thanked her for her kindness.

'I'll bet you're relieved about this rain,' Ann said to the waitress.

'We are, Signora. We will all be most thankful around here.'

Soon Luke and Ann were drying their faces before sipping white wine and nibbling grissini, prosciutto, cheese and olives.

'What will you do for the rest of the week?' Luke asked.

'Relax and read. Did you just postpone by a day?'

'Yes.'

There was a silence between them as the rain absorbed their gaze, still falling fast and causing large concentric circles on the sea water. The black clouds overhead moved only slowly now that the wind was gentle rather than gusty. Ann broke the silence.

'Do tell me to mind my own business but you said your wife died almost three years ago now. Are you coming up to an anniversary, then?'

'In seven weeks. On the ninth of November.' Luke replied.

'The ninth. The number nine. Sadly appropriate.'

'How?'

'It's the last single digit,' said Ann. 'Represents completion. Let me look it up on my phone again.' She took her mobile from her tote bag and googled the number nine before continuing: 'Yes. Here it is. "A culmination of wisdom and experience. Gives energy of both endings and new beginnings."'

'Really?' said Luke, cynicism in his voice. He suddenly felt a little guilty that he had slapped her down when she was trying to be helpful again. 'I'm sorry,' he said. 'I didn't mean to be so sarky.'

She smiled. 'How have the anniversaries been? Do you think it will feel any different this year?'

Luke was appreciating Ann's sensitivity and had begun to feel able, willing even, to open up to her just a little. She was an outsider, after all, and therefore safe. He could leave it all here, he thought, on his last day. Their encounter, offering him an outlet for his thoughts and feelings, seemed to fit in fortuitously with the reason behind this trip.

'Less intense last year than the first so maybe it won't feel so bloody debilitating this time,' he said. 'But the pain never goes away. It just… well, lurks in the shadows until you're vulnerable, feeling low, and then it strikes. You think you're making progress, feeling better – if better is the right word – and then there seems almost to be a guilt about feeling better. I mean, take today. It's been such a confluence of feelings. Sad at times, enjoyable at others. And then I think that it's wrong to enjoy myself. That Billie can't so I shouldn't.'

He looked across at Ann. She was sitting with an elbow on the table, her chin resting in her palm, listening intently to him.

'The first year was hideous,' he continued. 'I expected the sadness, but the sheer, undiluted madness of it all took me by surprise. The sitting on the landing at two in the morning, shouting and begging her to appear as some sort of ghost. Ringing her mobile number but just getting one long disconnected noise. Not even her voice telling you to leave a message. The regrets about things said and not said, done and not done. The open rawness of my emotions.'

He stopped himself. That was enough. 'But you don't want to hear all about that.'

'Actually, I do,' said Ann. 'I hope that doesn't sound too nosey. What I mean is, I would be happy to, if you wanted to talk about it. About her. Do you feel more able now to tell me what she was like?'

Luke took a long sip of wine. *What the hell*, he thought. *Talk about Billie? That's too good an opportunity to miss.*

'Smart. Big personality. Witty. Generous. Loving. Warm. Passionate. A very good TV producer who made some funny shows. And realistic and self-aware. She told me before she died that she wanted me to be honest in my eulogy at her funeral. So I'm not blackening her memory when I say she could also be unreasonable and quick to anger. Arsey, I think the modern word is. She wouldn't listen once the red mist came down and it could get quite scary. But then she was like a storm that would blow itself out, and she had a smile that meant you forgave her everything. She didn't hold grudges. Well, not in the short term. It was always a surprise what she remembered years down the line.'

Luke issued a short chuckle.

'She sounds a remarkable woman. What did she die of?' Ann ventured. "Do tell me to shut up…'

Luke took another long sip of his wine. Here, under this canopy where he had sat with Billie a dozen or so times over their holidays, he wondered himself what might come out next. He had spoken about it little by little to various close friends but not in one linked narrative really. The anonymity of this woman and her invitation to keep talking was appealing. He put on his sunglasses, though the sky was still dark.

'Secondary ovarian cancer,' he said. 'Which means it started there and spread. She lived for four years after her diagnosis. First off, she had chemo, six cycles of it, once every three weeks, and it worked. She tolerated it well, though it was debilitating. She'd be OK for a couple of days after each one, then exhausted and cold for a few days after that. *It's like a truck has hit me*, she used to say. She'd lie on the sofa with a blanket over her, watching daytime TV in between napping because it meant she could turn off her thoughts. Then she would get her energy back for a couple of weeks and go back to work before the whole routine started again. Steroids bloated her and she lost her hair, but I thought she looked more attractive than ever. Bandanas suited her.'

'She had good remission afterwards?' Ann enquired.

'For three years. Her hair grew back and she went back to her fighting weight. She worked pretty much as normal, though she'd get tired. In public she was strong, in private she was vulnerable, emotionally and physically. She had check-ups every three months, quarterly reprieves that we would celebrate. Then a blood test showed something wrong and a scan found that it had moved to her liver. She knew enough about cancer by then to recognise that when it spread to an organ, it was all a bit serious. She went back onto another chemo but it didn't work. After a couple of sessions, they scanned her and the tumours were growing. They changed to another drug but that didn't work either. We had nine months of this and then one day they told us that they had run out of treatment options and it was now a question of palliative care. Privately, unknown to her, I went to see her oncologist and asked how long she might have. Six months at the most, he said. She had four in the end. We came here for the final time a month after that prognosis, while we still could. When we got home afterwards, she grew less mobile, more bloated. She'd spike temperatures over forty degrees and I'd be taking her in and out of our local A and E so they could pump her full of saline and vitamins for a day or two and then send her home. Then came the last time in hospital and the last week of her life. The worst one of mine. They couldn't find veins strong enough to accept needles any more. She was so agitated and upset that I took her home. Maybe in hospital they could have kept her alive a bit longer but I wanted her to have the comfort of our home. I felt guilty, but then that's magical thinking really.'

'Magical thinking? What's that?' Ann asked.

'I didn't know either until... well, all of this. It's where those close to a deceased loved one believe that if they'd done something differently there might have been a different outcome. You might have been able to keep them alive, if only for a while.'

'But she had a terminal cancer. There was nothing you could do.'

'Yes. At the time, though, you mull everything over, turn every stone, wonder how you could have altered the course of it all. Now I know there's a big difference between extending life and extending death.'

Luke stopped. He drained his glass of wine. Ann reached for the bottle and poured him some more. He kept staring straight ahead at the harbour and the small boats bobbing on the surface. The rain was now puddling the dock.

'Anyway, I brought her home. She could walk no more. Not even with a stick. I took her out in a wheelchair a couple of times but she hated being seen in it. She hated being so… so reduced. It was November and the days were growing colder and darker. She just wanted to lie on a sofa and lose herself in trash telly. She struggled even to take in thin broth. She couldn't get up the stairs any more and a neighbour helped me bring a single bed downstairs for her. Her limbs were emaciated but her stomach was bloated with liquid. I couldn't cope any longer with her dying physical needs, much as I tried, and contacted the hospital. They arranged for local specialist nurses to come and tend to her. I was so relieved. They did things I didn't know about to soothe her situation. They syringed water into her mouth to keep her hydrated. Gave her liquid morphine. Put flavoured ice cubes on her tongue. And they included me, for which I will ever be grateful. I washed her face. I brushed her hair. During the nights, before she fell into a coma, she would want music played or a TV news channel on in the background. Just so she could hear voices, I think. The silence and the blackness of the night must have terrified her.'

Luke took off his sunglasses and buried his head in his hands for a moment before looking back out at the harbour again and putting his shades back on. He had no need to wear them in this light but they helped to dim the starkness of his visions.

'Honestly, if you've had enough…' Ann said. But Luke had not. He was going to take this opportunity.

'I became exhausted, awake most of the night with her. I didn't want to sleep in case she wanted something. I could nap during the days when the nurses came in for an hour or two but

I wanted every moment with her I could. One afternoon, a nurse told me to go and have a nap upstairs. I wasn't doing her any favours by being tired, they said. I needed to be fresher for her. I drifted off for a couple of hours but then there was a knock at the bedroom door. Billie's breathing had begun to change, the nurse said. I dashed downstairs and sat with her. I was worried that she would be in some pain, but thankfully she was still just about swallowing the morphine the nurse could get into her mouth through a plastic syringe. I was frightened – for myself, if I'm honest – that there would be some terrifying death rattle. But there wasn't. After a couple of hours, with me talking to her and mopping her forehead with a flannel, her breathing slowed to a halt and she just... just expired. I looked at the nurse and said: "Has she gone?" She looked at me and said: "We need to wait ten minutes before I write the official time of death to be sure, but yes, she's gone." I was numb. I had done plenty of crying but I couldn't at that moment. A doctor came to the house for some paperwork formalities and the nurse went off shift and all of a sudden I was left with Billie. Just me and her again. Except only one of us was breathing. It sounds ghoulish, I know, but in that moment, I understood these weird stories about people who keep a corpse in their house for a long time. I couldn't bear to let her go. I just sat there at her bedside, talking to her until the room began to darken with the late afternoon. I came out of some sort of trance and phoned the undertaker. Thirty minutes later, I was taking the advice of a man with a kind face and sitting in a different room while they carried her out in a body bag, I guess, to whatever vehicle they had outside. Ten minutes after that, I was wandering from room to room in a house that had been just right for two, and the occasional guest, like my son, and too big for one. She was gone. Gone for good. I've never understood that expression. What's good about it? At that moment, it was all bad.'

Luke looked across at Ann. She was wiping a tear from her eye. He took a handkerchief from his pocket and handed it to her.

'You really loved her, didn't you?' she said between sobs.

'Yes. Yes, I did,' said Luke. 'She could be bloody infuriating but, my God, she was magnificent.'

'You miss her, of course. And I suspect you always will.'

Suddenly Luke let out a long, loud howl and the odd tear that had moistened his eyes turned into a torrent. The waitress came in search of the source of the disturbing noise and saw Luke weeping uncontrollably. Ann caught her eye, smiled and shook her head before the woman could say something. The waitress nodded and retreated. Ann reached across the table and took Luke's hand in hers. With the other hand, she offered him the handkerchief he had given her and he took it. He dabbed his eyes.

'I am so sorry,' he said between sobs. 'This is so undignified. I don't know what's come over me.'

'Absolutely no need to apologise,' Ann said. 'Dignity is very overrated.' There was a pause and she withdrew her hand from his. 'Excuse me. I just need the loo,' she added, rising suddenly and disappearing into the bar.

When she returned, Luke thanked her for giving him a moment alone. Actually, she said, it was she who needed a moment alone. He said he would go in and pay the bill for the wine, which they had now finished, but she said it was taken care of. That was most kind of her, he said.

'Thank you for telling me all of that,' Ann said. 'I feel very privileged that you felt able to.'

'It's I who should be thanking you for listening,' Luke replied. 'I hope I didn't – what's the parlance now? – overshare?'

They both smiled and made eye contact for a moment before Luke turned away.

'Well, it looks like the rain has eased enough at least for us to head back to the hotel, and time is marching on,' he said. 'What's more, I think I could do with a long soak in a hot bath.'

Dusk was working its way from the harbour mouth and into the narrow streets that rose above them. Without words passing between them as they contemplated the enormous intimacy that Luke had risked, they slowly walked the kilometre or so back to the hotel. By the time they were almost there, the dribble of lingering rain had ceased.

Halfway across the hotel car park, they were stopped in their tracks by raised voices. The Scandinavian couple stood at the entrance to the hotel, clearly angry with each other, gesticulating furiously, conducting two monologues that would not be heard by the other. Ann and Luke could pick up only a little of what was being said but it was certainly not screaming of harmony. When the couple saw Ann and Luke, they stopped arguing, nodded and smiled. Each took the other's hand and they began to walk towards the town.

'Hello, Ann,' they both said as they passed.

'Hello,' she replied.

'Mr and Mrs Not-So-Perfect-After-All,' said Luke when they'd moved out of earshot.

'It's Kurt and Freya,' said Ann. 'I've got to know them a little bit. They're all right actually. From Malmo. Didn't expect that though. They seemed so together and devoted. People surprise you, don't they?'

Inside the hotel lobby, the manager Massimo was arguing with a receptionist behind the desk, trying to keep his voice down but clearly animated. He stopped when he saw Luke and Ann coming through the door. The English couple sat together on a sofa, saying nothing as usual, both savouring gin and tonics. They were people-watching, though with few people around, Ann and Luke piqued their interest instantly. Especially when, having collected their respective keys from Massimo at the desk, there was now an awkwardness to them as they stood in the middle of the reception area. Ann and Luke had shared a memorable day – and the most pleasant but also deepest and saddest conversations either of them had experienced in almost three years – but it felt like their time together had reached a conclusion, despite it being only early evening. Neither wanted any more food or drink. Both had said all they needed or wanted to. To continue this encounter would be to risk diluting the content of the day.

'Well, goodnight then,' said Ann.

'Goodnight,' he replied.

'Have a pleasant trip home.'

'Thank you.'

She reached into her tote bag and pulled out a purse. She took out a business card and handed it to Luke. He took it and stared down at it.

'That's got my email address and phone number on it.'

'Oh right, thank you.'

She stood there for a moment, waiting. Then she leant forward, kissed him on the cheek, turned and walked away.

'Ann,' he called. She turned and took a couple of steps back towards him.

'Yes?'

'I was wondering…'

'Yes?'

'That pink velour tracksuit you wear when out walking in the mornings… Forgive me, but it doesn't, well, feel like you. You are an intelligent, attractive woman and –'

'Is that a compliment? Thank you.'

'You're welcome… Well, you are, but that wasn't my first impression when you spoke to me that morning, I have to say. Because of that tracksuit, I think.'

Ann smiled. 'It was a Christmas gift from Amy, my little granddaughter. My daughter said she saw it in a shop and Amy said that it would be perfect for Granny. You're right, it's not really me, but I am fond of it because it reminds me of her and makes me smile. The trainers came from my daughter. "Might as well embrace, it mum," she said.'

Luke smiled at her and nodded. Ann waited a moment before returning a smile. When it was clear there was going to be no more conversation, she turned again for the staircase and Luke watched her disappear.

He looked again at her business card, his over-zealous study of it interrupted by a voice in the corner.

'Excuse me,' said the English man, beckoning Luke over.

'My name is Johnson. Eddie Johnson. This is Thelma, my wife.'

The woman said hello and took a sip of her gin and tonic. Luke responded with a hello of his own.

''Ere, sit down for moment,' said Eddie.

Luke did as he was bidden. Eddie asked if he would like a drink but Luke declined, saying he needed to get back to his room. Eddie was not diverted, however.

'Eh, you know that German couple that were here over the weekend?'

'Um. Yes. I did notice them,' Luke replied.

'They've only gone and done a runner without paying.'

'What?'

'Yes. Poor old Massimo is beside himself.'

'How strange,' said Luke. 'They looked pretty well off to me. They were drinking Dom Pérignon.'

'Ah well,' said Eddie. 'There's having money and there's the illusion of having money, if you know what I mean. Thankfully, we have money, don't we, Thelma? Was in at the start of mobile phones.' He winked and tapped his nose.

Luke rose and was about to make his escape when Eddie grabbed his right forearm and leaned forward conspiratorially.

'I hope you don't mind me asking this, but are you a widower?'

Luke was taken aback but found himself, out of politeness, answering almost before he considered the effrontery of the question.

'Well, yes I am actually.'

'I thought you were. I said you looked like a widower, didn't I, Thelma? Well, you said you thought he was as well, didn't you?'

'I did, yes,' said Thelma.

'Ann is a very nice woman,' said Eddie. 'We've got to know and like her since we've been here. We live in Croydon. Not too far from her. We might meet up with her.'

'Yes, she is very nice,' said Luke.

'We thought you and her might make a nice couple.'

Luke issued a flickering smile and said he really needed to get back to his room.

'But before I go, do you mind if I ask *you* a question?' he said, attempting to change the subject.

'Course not. But I may not be able to answer it,' said Eddie. He laughed.

'I see you two at breakfast, and around the hotel. I never see you speaking to each other.'

Thelma laughed. 'Simple explanation for that,' she said. 'I love him to bits and he loves me to bits. But we couldn't bear talking to each other all the time, could we, love?'

'No,' said Eddie. 'If you ask me, the problem with marriage these days is communication. There's too much of it.' He laughed and Thelma joined in.

'We're not really the chatty types,' Eddie added. 'We're just comfortable in each other's company. Just lookers and listeners, aren't we, precious?'

He reached across the table and took Thelma's hand. She leant forward and kissed him on the lips.

'Good to hear that,' said Luke, getting up and bidding them goodnight.

He ascended the staircase. It was barely 7pm, but it felt like it had been a long day. He had said many things. Ann had said many things too, but one sentence stuck in his mind: people surprise you, don't they?

Dear Adam,

Thank you so much for meeting up with me last week. I know it took a lot for you to agree to see me again after all these years, and after everything that happened between you, me and even Christine, but I think and hope it was worth all the soul-searching on your part about whether it was wise. I certainly felt it helped me deal with some demons from my past and move on in my life. I am grateful for that opportunity.

Hope I didn't look too gruesome. I've put on some weight after the chemo, mainly due to the steroids, and my hair is growing back too slowly for my liking. I appreciate you saying you liked my hair as it was like a buzz cut, but I'm not so sure. It's still coming back only in patches. I'd like it to be a bit longer and more 'normal'. Must say, you looked well. Italy obviously agrees with you.

In some ways, strange as this may sound, I have come to feel some gratitude for the cancer. As I told you, it has made me re-evaluate my life. It most definitely gives you a focus on what is important and what is frivolous, what needs to be let go of and what needs to be clung to tightly. Acrimony and resentment from the past is certainly something that I need to be free of. And apologising, making amends, for things I said and did has become paramount for me.

One day, perhaps, even Christine might permit me to say sorry to her in person but I'll understand if not, and I do get why you wanted to keep our meeting just between us. I'd be grateful if you'd do the same for me. It's not that I have anything to hide from Luke, it's more that I don't want to have to go into too much detail about my past with you, or other men around that time, when my present and future is firmly committed to him. I just don't want to do anything that might jeopardise that and I think he is a bit sensitive about these things.

I know now that you knew I wasn't always faithful to you. That first summer I went to Switzerland, for example, I did meet a boy there that I quite liked, as you discerned. I'm sorry I wasn't more specific last week and I still don't want to go into too much detail, but I was embarrassed when we met up in Paris that September. All I can say is that he was certainly not a patch on you and I was very young, still a teenager, and less mature than you.

There were other times in my twenties, to be honest. Someone at the TV station I met up with now and then after work. Of course, I felt bad about it at the time but I look back and have to be realistic. I can't judge myself from a position of more mature insight, though I do apologise to you. Judging you by my own standards, I thought you were having an affair a couple of times because of your distance, and I was angry with you when you hooked up with Christine. I just didn't believe you that you hadn't been seeing her when we were together, but I now accept your word that you weren't.

I – in fact we – always have to remember that I was eight years younger than you. You were my first real relationship, apart from a couple of dates and drunken snogs and fumbles with dopey sixth-form blokes at school. When I met you, you'd been out with several other women already and were ready for something more solid and satisfying. I thought I was, but I hadn't realised that I needed to have other experiences before I was ready to settle down. And I hadn't realised, coming from where I did and that era, that sex could be enjoyed as a woman. Wolverhampton in the early 1980s was more about avoiding it in case some loser got you pregnant and ruined the rest of your life.

It was only when I met Luke really that I was ready to settle, though I hadn't thought of it as clinically as that. He wasn't exactly on the rebound, as he'd been separated a year earlier and his divorce had come through, but he was still a little bit of a sad figure. Which was strange to me, given that he was a comedy writer. He came up with all this funny material but he seemed so wounded. Tears of a clown, and all that. Maybe that was what attracted me, a man who made me laugh and who was vulnerable too. Light and shade. Shallow and deep.

He made me want to be faithful to him, Adam. And I think, having turned thirty, I was finally ready. After you, I had other flings with telly people but nothing lasting. Nobody I wanted to be with for more than a few weeks. I liked that Luke introduced me to his son quickly and the three of us got on. Jude sensed from a young age that I could make his dad happy again and he was desperate to have a happy dad back.

I know you saw me as high maintenance. God, I bloody hate that phrase. As if blokes can't be hard work. Luke has been and I love him for that. He has his moods, can be sullen and difficult, angry and shouty, but then I can too. I love him because all those moods are part of who he is. Lob in his wit and his willingness to bare his soul emotionally, and he quickly became 'the one' I wanted to commit to.

And let me tell you this in confidence Adam, quite a few men have wanted to sleep with me even since I've been with Luke, even since our marriage. None of them would ever have wanted anything more than sex, I'm certain of that. Luke has been the only one since you who ever wanted to stay with me. And he's been the only one I would ever have wanted to stay with. A quick roll – even with a star of one production I was on, which was flattering – was not for me. And I'm proud to say that of myself now, given previous experiences. Sex does so often get mixed up with love, and the two are quite different and separate. Women realise that. I'm not sure too many men do.

I'm happy that you've found something meaningful and lasting with Christine too. My jealousy – which spilled out as anger – has long since departed. I'm going to repeat what I said to you last week: that time I came into the university, and my outburst there, was totally unacceptable and I am so sorry. Please pass that on to Christine, if ever you do feel able to tell her about us meeting. Blimey, cancer really is compromising my hard woman image, isn't it?

It's now time to get on and make the most of what time I have left. The ovarian cancer is a secondary, which – as I explained to you but many people can't grasp – means that it has spread from its original site and there is no cure, only a series of treatments that bring life extension. This chemo will have done that for now but I live from one three-month hospital check-up to another when I go back for blood tests and they scan me if needs be.

Thank you too for your recommendation of the Hotel Miramare in Recoli. I am going to book it for this summer. I hope the treatment and the steroids that I have to stay on will continue to work so that I have enough energy to be able to savour some sun, sea and seafood. Along with the mutual love and companionship of Luke, whom I have given a hard time sometimes but who has made me a better person. This bloody disease will get me in the end unfortunately and Luke will be left on his own, but I aim to make what remains of our time together memorable. I shall be bloody upset if he finds somebody else when I'm gone. Ha ha. Actually, there is a bit of truth in that but there will come a time when he will tire of his loneliness, I suspect, and in all seriousness, I wouldn't begrudge him a new relationship.

I will forever know that I was the love of his life. He told me that in the little consulting room at the hospital after the oncologist had delivered my diagnosis. Then he was sorry he had said it, bless him, as 'it sounds a bit final when of course we have plenty of time, don't we?' I knew I was the love of his life anyway. Because nobody else could have put up with me for all this time and kept bouncing back. Somebody once said we were indestructible and we are. Sorry to break it to you, Adam (ha ha again!), but he has been the love of my life, too.

Love still, in a purely platonic, water-under-the-bridge, thanks-for-the-memories kind of way. Wish me well in my Camden cancer (one consolation is they do sell colourful bandanas at the market). I wish you and Christine well in your Italian idyll.

(God I think this may be the longest email I've ever written. Sorree.)

Billie

9

Luke had been saving the opening of the thin rectangular wooden crate that had arrived ten days ago for this day, the ninth of November. At 6.30am, he found his claw hammer, carefully eased out the nails holding the hard protective structure together and gently parted the wood. After that, he carefully cut through the sticky tape binding the bubble wrap and there stood the painting all its glory. Luke held it up in front of him, tears springing to his eyes. It was stunning.

He set it on a chair and read the accompanying note: 'Signor Jessop. It has been a pleasure working on this for you in honour of your late wife. I hope *The Terrace at Recoli* gives you pleasure too. Adriano.' Luke would email Adriano Montelli tomorrow to say, that it most certainly would give him pleasure. He had been so warm when Luke contacted him: *'A print? I am happy to paint you an original if you give me the dimensions. I will give you an acceptable price.'* It was more than acceptable, and worth every Euro.

Luke hung the painting in the living room opposite the door, so that he would see it every time he walked into the room and could view it constantly from his armchair. It was a replica of that scene by the breakfast room at the Miramare but with the colours heightened. *'I want bright and vivacious to mirror my Billie,'* he had told Adriano. When he stepped back to admire the work, Luke saw that it was slightly askew – a drawback of being single with no-one to guide you. Like gauging the amount of peas for one person. Luke couldn't be bothered to care just now. He would straighten the picture another time. For now, it was perfect and he felt flushed with satisfaction as he dried his eyes for the second weep of a commemorative day that usually brought many tears.

'There you go, Billie. How do you like that?' he said. 'We'll always have Recoli.'

He had resolved today to repeat the solitary routine of the first and second anniversaries that had enabled him at least to function without crumbling into a physical and emotional heap. He drove to his favourite florist to assemble a large bouquet of pink lilies and red and white roses, picking them one by one with the assistant. He liked the expense of it all and the feel of it being a special occasion, rather than buying supermarket flowers. It showed that it meant something.

It was the same with the headstone that he had chosen for her grave. The shiny images of garish memorials in the brochures that the undertakers had given him just did not feel right for her; they just looked so cheap. He wanted something plain and simple, and was sure that Billie would have done too. Online, Luke found an expert stonemason in the Cotswolds who worked in Welsh slate and he made a special trip to agree a design. The result was slim, elegant and memorable, just as he'd wanted to reflect her. After listing her name and dates, just one other word was engraved: *Treasured*. Everybody admired it. It stood tall and proud in the plot that he had bought for her at Highgate Cemetery, in a leafy nook by an old dry stone wall and with the branches of an oak holding her in its enduring solidity. He had wanted somewhere reverential, impressive both for her and for him to visit, where he could sit with her in a sheltered environment of peace, communicate with her in silent privacy.

In the days and early months after her funeral, he visited almost daily, though the winter cold limited his time there. Come the spring and summer, he would sit in a folding chair and read a book several times a week, punctuating his stay with his one-way conversation with Billie.

Today he was relieved that it was fine, if chilly. He had brought her favourite tall yellow vase and filled it with water from the tap at the cemetery entrance. Having become expert in flower-arranging by now, he carefully positioned the roses and lilies and placed the vase into a small hollow he created at the foot of the headstone of the turfed grave. It made for a pleasing tableau. He thought she would be pleased too.

He unfolded the chair at the foot of the grave and took his seat. He was wrapped up in a Barbour coat and her favourite beige cashmere scarf. He took a thermos flask from a holdall and poured himself a coffee.

'So my darling, what's new with you? Anything going on there? Producing anything decent? Nothing much happening here. Jake rang me about maybe joining a writers' room for a new sitcom pilot he's directing but I still can't fit the two parts of mo and jo together, I'm afraid. I wish I was more worried but I'm not. In fact, I'm not worried about much these days. Should I be worried about not being worried, do you think? I mean, I'm not even terrified of death any longer really. I'm grateful to you for that, of course. I think you've taught me how to die. I know you were angry for a month or so when they told you there was no more treatment they could give you, but I can see now that anger was your way of showing that you were actually frightened. We got to Recoli one last time though, didn't we, and that helped. After that, there seemed to be a serenity, an acceptance to you. That was such an example to me. When the worst thing in life actually happens, there's nothing left to fear, and more head room to consider the important things in life. I think

I've reached a point where I can deal with outcomes either way. What I mean is, if something bad happens, or even something good, these days I don't get too upset or excited by any of it. It's all the same to me. Balance, perhaps. Or maybe it's a sign that I just don't care. Maybe it's some kind of acceptance. Who can say? What does get to me, my darling, is ageing. You're lucky to be free of all that, I can tell you. What a stupid thing to say. Of course you're not lucky. You'd have wanted to grow old. I wanted you to grow old. Us together. You passed the ultimate test when men come out of their sex-obsessed days and think about relationships: can you grow old with this woman? It's all very well for Stevie Nicks to sing about the slow, graceful flow of age but she was bloody young when she wrote that. She didn't know anything about back and joint ache and getting up to piss three times a night. Or a penis that withers. It's a muscle, you know. And muscles wither through lack of exercise. You know, there were so many times I wished you didn't have such ready answers for things, so many things to say. So many times I got annoyed that I wasn't allowed to finish my sentences. Since you went, there have been so many times when I'd have given anything to hear you answer back, so many questions I've wanted answering.'

There was a gust of wind through the trees and a few of the remaining leaves on the oak fell at his feet. Luke looked down at them.

'Ah, so you do have something to say for yourself. I do hear your voice now and then but it's what I imagine you saying. I thought you might find my withering plight faintly amusing. It's not about ageing so much. It's more about loss. Quite apart from you. Your body loses its… well, reliability. My energy levels are so much lower. Anyway, enough feeling sorry for myself. What's it like where you are? Any better than here? I do bloody hope so. I mean, it's OK. It's not a bad life. It just has a huge you-sized hole in it. I feel apart from – instead of a part of – things a lot of the time. I see Jude now and then but he's got his own life, of course. New girlfriend, too, and you'll know how much time that requires. Not just physically but in having your mind occupied by nothing and nobody else. Well, it sounds familiar to me, Billie. I read, I shop, I cook. I go for walks. I watch movies. I listen to our music. People talk about seizing the day and making the most of things but I don't think it means flying around the world or paying fortunes for "experiences". I think it means being present in the moment, with a person or two to sustain your soul and doing activities that nourish your spirit.

'I have to admit, though, that life just isn't exciting any more like it was with you, and it doesn't feel like it will ever be again. I'll have to accept that, I suppose. But I so want to see you again. I'm less obsessed now by wanting to start again with you and re-do it all, this time without the arguments and regrets. A pipe dream, I know, that life together a second time around would be less... what, contested? We were who we were and our passions and intensity were what made us attractive to each other. I do think of the future more but beyond this life's future. Will I get to see you where you are? Is there a "where you are" or is it just a black hole? Am I talking into a void here, Billie, or not? Are people in physical form? Lots of religious people believe that it's something deeper, a reconnection of souls together in harmony for eternity. Others reckon that I have to let go of you for you to pass on to your next life, your next assignment and allocation of a physical form. Is that true? I would hate to think I'm holding you back. Or would I hate that? I mean, I don't want you to meet someone else in a new life. No, that's mean. Apologies for my jealousies and insecurities. It's about me and not you, though even if I am embarrassed about them, it doesn't mean the anxiety around them isn't real. Do you feel that about me meeting someone? People tell me you would want me to, but I tell them that they didn't know you properly. It gets a laugh. The only laugh I *have* got for a while.

'Been thinking a lot lately about that article I read about pilgrimage when you're grieving a loved one. You know, the one I told you about a while back. That going to places you shared helps to reconnect with happy memories and to honour them. Even let go. I don't know if that's true. I don't think I ever will – or want to – let go. But I think often about my trip to Recoli and there you were. And weren't. All I know is that I missed you like crazy. I also read that you should go back and laugh in places where you've cried. Sounds nice and simple, doesn't it? Like a lot of this trite grief advice. Grief. It feels like it's become my bloody hobby sometimes. I ended up crying in places where we'd laughed. What I haven't told you is that I did meet someone there, Billie. She was nice; I liked her. But I don't know. It just felt… wrong. I thought I might be betraying you. Cheating, almost. I also made it pretty plain that you were the love of my life and that there was never going to be anyone else like you. That probably put her off, anyway. Along with my hair going from grey to white rather rapidly now. And this bloody spare tyre that I can't seem to get rid of. What? What do you mean I need to exercise? Don't you bloody start. I tell myself that enough. All right, I'll go for a long walk. I always do on the anniversary, don't I?

'That's enough talking for today. They say that I'll stop talking to you one day. But I can't see it happening. Goodbye for now, though, my love.'

He blew a kiss towards her headstone, gathered up his flask, holdall and chair and headed back to the car. He drove to Primrose Hill, found a parking space and opted to walk down into Regent's Park. The top of the Hill offered one of the best views of the central London skyline in the city and he marvelled again at the magnificence of the modern capital, of the Shard, the

London Eye and the BT Tower, before walking down towards the zoo. He wanted to reflect, yes, but when that grew too draining, he wanted also to see signs of life. He was ready for that now after his cemetery solitude. Around the zoo there was always a bustle, even at this time of year. Excited youngsters reached for their mothers' hands. Couples walked arm in arm. Life continued. Love persisted.

As he walked, south along The Broad Walk towards Euston Road, he sought to compare how he had felt last year, and that first year. Those anniversaries had brought visceral, then gentle, sobbing. Today thus far was more quietly melancholic, the only tears those of pleasure at the painting. He appreciated that the passing of time had taken away the rawness of the pain, but cursed that same passing of time for its potential to blur the sharpness of his memories, worrying that he would tire of memories, that they would grow dim and would not be enough to sustain him. He soothed himself with the thought that the anger he had felt at her dying – and all this misery he had put himself through (which was nothing compared to her suffering and fate, he guiltily told himself) – was now dissipating. He replayed his conversation with Adam that day in Recoli and reconnected with his relief that many questions had been answered, even if he still wondered on bad days whether there was a truth... and then a whole truth.

Luke walked for half an hour around the Queen Mary's Rose Gardens and the lake, the wind bringing water to his eyes, and then back up to his car on Primrose Hill Road as the light was fading. That was enough for one day. Home to turn the heating on, to tea and crumpets – or pikelets, as Billie always insisted on calling them. He did like this time of year. The cold and darkness were not demanding in the way the lighter months were. They almost insisted that you made the most of the longer days, got out and about, did things, were sociable. The onset of winter gave you permission to hide away and ignore the clamour of sympathisers, many of whom were slipping away now that the open wound of his grief had been dressed and he had become less obviously messy or in need of fixing. He had to admit his own part in all that. Considering himself self-contained and sufficient, he had withdrawn into his own company the majority of the time.

Within an hour of being home, warmth and nourishment had unfrozen his brain and Luke felt a modicum of peace, a gratitude for times remembered rather than resentment that there would be no more with her. He decided it was time to check his mobile, which he had turned off for the day. Some nice texts from old friends who remembered him, and Billie, on this date. One from Jude saying he would be on his phone if you wanted to talk, Dad.

He turned on the laptop to check his emails, which were so much harder to read on a mobile. They were mostly junk – companies from whom he might have bought the odd thing and who retained his email address. He really needed to remember to unsubscribe. Then he noticed one from an unusual source. In fact, it was the first time the name of Adam Byrne had ever come up in his emails. The subject head was: Billie. He opened it immediately and devoured its content.

Hi Luke,

I know today is the third anniversary of Billie's death and I just thought I would make contact to let you know that I've been thinking about you. In fact, I've been thinking about a lot of things since we met almost two months ago now. Mainly I've been debating with myself whether to forward you an email that Billie wrote to me a week after she came to see me that time I told you about.

I thought at first that it should be a quid pro quo, that one good turn deserves another, after you gave me the box with those letters from me to her.

And despite all that I said about secrets that partners keep from each other, and perhaps even should for the avoidance of conflict, I did – very nervously – tell Christine about them. What you said as we parted, about secrets that you and Billie may have kept from each other and now there was no way of knowing certain things, really hit home with me.

Anyway, I told her that I had met up with Billie in Genoa and then you in Recoli. And that I'd read the letters you gave me and they were like antique maps of places with names no longer recognisable, a book set in a different era that had nothing to say to me about modern times. I was certainly detached from the two characters involved. Time changes so much, doesn't it? For all the conflict between me, Billie and Christine, I will always be grateful that I met her. If I hadn't known Billie and we hadn't moved to take up jobs in the same location, I wouldn't have met Christine, would I? Christine was a little hurt and angry for a day or so that I'd kept things from her but then she forgave me, saying she accepted that it was part of my past I needed to acknowledge. I rediscovered what a remarkable woman she is.

But I digress... I then thought that you believed that the box should belong to me, quite laudably. Billie's email to me was different, though. It was personal and private. I considered this. Then it occurred to me that there might have been a greater good at work. You were clearly over the worst of your grief but you seemed, if you don't mind me saying so, a little stuck. As if you were in some place between

129

a despair that had eased and a hope that might be calling you. Torn and confused. Functioning but at half capacity.

Hence me having decided to forward the email from Billie to me, below, on to you. I hope it brings you comfort, solace and that hope, Luke. I knew today would be difficult for you and I thought it would be a good day to send it. God, she loved you, you know. We were both lucky that she gave the two of us her time and love, given that she was like trying to nail jelly to a wall sometimes. But in the end it was luckier for you, as it was meant to be, just as Christine and me was meant to be. You were 'the one' for Billie. Never again doubt that.

Regards,
Adam

Luke devoured Billie's email to Adam, reading aloud what he saw as highlights.

A man who made me laugh and was vulnerable too…

He made me want to be faithful to him…

He's been the only one I would ever have wanted to stay with…

He's been the love of my life.

Over and over he read it. His heart raced. He printed it off and folded it into quarters so that it would fit into a leather wallet in which he kept special mementos – his favourite picture of her, and his favourite picture of them together, along with a message on a picture postcard of the church that she had given to him the night before their wedding: *Looks like we made it. Don't be late. That's my prerogative. B xxx*

Once he had dried his eyes –the tears now more of love and relief rather than sorrow and loss – he had a couple of things he needed to do. First, he had ten diaries to dispose of in the recycling bin. Then he returned to his laptop. He had an email to compose.

*

The South Bank was thronged with people lured by the myriad, mingling aromas of a German market. Christmas was still five weeks away but anticipation was in the crisp early-afternoon air, fuelled by the sweet, sickly scents of doughnuts and the savoury smells of bratwurst coming from what were supposed to be Teutonic huts but resembled garden sheds.

Luke grew agitated as he stood at the base of Hungerford Bridge. This had been his and Billie's territory. There was the National Theatre where they had been members, over there the Festival Hall where she'd bought tickets for some soul-touching classical concerts. Not far along the river was Tate Modern, which she loved, especially the members' terrace looking out on to St Paul's. He just didn't feel right being here.

And then he saw her, walking towards him with a smile on her face.

'Hello, you,' Ann said.

'Hello,' Luke replied.

There was a moment of awkwardness, neither knowing whether to shake hands, hug or just smile at each other. Ann moved towards him, gave him a loose hug and a brief kiss on the cheek. He was grateful that she had assumed the role of icebreaker.

'So what's it to be?' she asked. 'Coffee and a sandwich at the National, maybe? That foyer is so special, isn't it? Walk along the South Bank up to Blackfriars, maybe?'

Luke had agreed to meet here because Ann's train from Putney came into Waterloo and he was familiar with the territory.

But that was now the issue for him. He knew the foyer of the National was special, and that the view on the walk along the river to Blackfriars was spectacular. He had been to both with Billie so often.

'I wonder if we could go somewhere, um… new?' he said. 'New to me, anyway.'

'Sure.' She thought for a moment. 'There's some nice gardens on the Embankment opposite and there's a sweet little café there. We can even sit outside and pretend the weather is healthily bracing rather than plain bloody cold.'

'Perfect,' said Luke.

They walked over Hungerford Bridge, taking in the view down to Tower Bridge that never grew tired nor failed to inspire awe and Ann led him into the gardens by Embankment tube station. He did not know, he said, how he had gone all these years without knowing this haven existed. Here they were in a green bubble separate from the bustle of the city surrounding them: Trafalgar Square to the north, the Houses of Parliament to the west and New Scotland Yard to the east. Across the river, they could see the National, controversially brutalist back in its 1970s conception but now an old, much-loved fixture that could be lit in various colours at night. Both it, and the charming curved roof of the Festival Hall, seemed distant now to Luke.

Luke bought some coffee and sandwiches from the café and took them out to the table that Ann had found.

'Best I could do,' he said. 'Cheese or chicken?'

'Looks good to me,' she replied. 'Chicken, please.'

They sipped and ate.

'Thank you for coming,' he said.

'Bit formal…' she teased.

'Sorry,' he said, and they both laughed.

'I didn't think I'd hear from you again,' said Ann.

'Well, been a bit busy. Things on. You know.'

She nodded.

'I did feel a bit of an idiot handing my contact details over to you in Recoli and standing there waiting for something back,' said Ann, having finished a mouthful.

'Sorry about that. It was gauche of me, wasn't it?' Luke replied.

'Yes. It was,' she said, clearly determined not to let him off the hook. 'So what made you contact me?'

'Well, I did enjoy our day at San Pietro. And I liked you.'

'I liked you too. You seemed like a decent man.'

'Thank you. Unlike Carlo?'

'Please...'

'Apologies,' said Luke. 'And if I was a bit curt and cold at times. I just... well, I just didn't feel ready for any kind of relationship.'

'Bit forward there. I'm not sure I was offering one.'

A look of horror came over Luke's face.

'Sorry. Have I misread things?'

'I'm teasing again. You'll get used to me. Or maybe you won't. Maybe nothing will happen. Maybe it will.' She paused and took a sip of coffee. 'Look, I took a risk. When you didn't contact me, I just put it down to experience. Your loss.'

'I'm sorry. I'm just not good at this dating thing.'

'This is a date?' she said.

'Well...,' Luke began to reply before seeing a mischievous look on Ann's face. 'Teasing, yes?'

She nodded. 'So you've not been out with anyone since your wife died?'

'Not really. I've had women friends – some friends of Billie's really – that I've had odd dinners or cinema visits with. You know, people I can do something with but not people I can do nothing with. They fall away with time. It happens. And one or two women I used to know that I rekindled friendships with. There's an attraction and a fascination with a messed-up widower, I think, but it palls for people. They drift away. And for my part, I'm always frightened that if I get close to a woman, given my experiences, she'll let me down. Or maybe it's me, rather than the situation.'

'We'll see,' said Ann. 'That's it?'

'There was a Saturday night when I'd had a glass of white too many and checked out an over-fifties dating site. It was horrifying, to be honest. Women in their fifties and sixties posting pictures of themselves in their forties. Some looked so desperate.'

'And of course men don't do that?'

'Touché,' he said and took another sip of coffee. 'To be honest, I thought you'd realised how much I loved Billie and you may have thought that nobody was going to compare. That anyone after her was just going to be next best.'

'God, men think they are so good at second-guessing women, don't they? I was actually very touched by what you had to say about you and her. It was very beautiful. And we all have a past. A past that involves loved ones, the like of which we may never meet again or feel the same about when we do meet someone.'

'And that doesn't put you off? I mean, that's quite a depressing thought, isn't it?'

'I don't think love is finite. It doesn't fit neatly into a bottle. It expands. There's enough to go around. You still love Billie and always will, yes?'

'Yes.'

'That's understandable. But it doesn't mean there isn't room in your heart for another. You remember that day at the bar when it was hosing down with rain and you poured your heart out?'

'Of course, I do.'

'What I actually thought was that if he could love a person like that, maybe he could love someone else like that too.'

She smiled at him and he smiled back.

'I've had to grieve too, you know,' she said.

There was a pause before she discerned that Luke was interested in this.

'My husband didn't die but I lost him. And I lost him to a younger woman. That was humiliating. I'm not going to be so crass as to say that at least you didn't have to suffer that. You suffered much worse. But it took me some years of misery before I got my self-respect back.'

'Do you not fear getting hurt again? I mean, I'm terrified. I can live in quiet contemplation and solitude quite comfortably, even if I can get twitchy when I start to realise that I'm comfortable and distrust the comfort. But I've had so much sadness, through a first marriage where she walked off with someone, and then Billie's death. I can't be hurt or abandoned again, even if Billie didn't abandon me deliberately. I just don't think I have the resilience left in me.'

'Resilience is another overvalued quality,' said Ann. 'Everybody has it. It's just keeping going after something bad happens. We don't have much choice, do we?'

'Billie used to say things like that.'

'Sooner or later, we all have to take a risk. You might get hurt. I might get hurt. Life's messy. But I'm determined not to petrify before my time.'

She reached across the bistro table and put a hand on top of his.

'We all have baggage and trauma, especially at our ages. I don't think they ever go away. Too many people make that mistake of thinking we're all going to be healed. Instead, I think we just have to learn to live with them. Find a way of accepting them. Learning to walk with a limp.'

Luke found himself moved. He nodded.

'Maybe all we can do is end up with the right regrets,' Ann added.

'That's good. Where did you get that?'

'Arthur Miller.'

'Marilyn Monroe's husband?'

'Well, he was a bit more that than. But it's nice that a bloke's considered an appendage for a change. Listen, too many people don't risk a next step because they'd rather stay stuck in something familiar. It may be painful, but there's comfort in the familiar. You have to acknowledge the past but keep going. We should visit the graveyard but not live there.'

Luke took this in for a minute.

'Have you had therapy?' he asked.

'Yes.'

'I thought so.'

'Have you?'

'No.'

'I thought not.'

Luke laughed. 'I have, I think, worked a fair bit of stuff out, though. I'm genuinely no longer frightened of death.'

'Which is liberating,' Ann said. 'It frees you to live.'

'Thank you,' he said.

There was a silence between them for a minute.

'I'm fifty-seven by the way,' Ann said, and they both laughed. 'Fifty-eight a week before Christmas. Your sixtieth this year sounded a bit low key so perhaps we could have a joint celebration. Go somewhere nice and expensive.'

'Possibly. Might make a nice change,' said Luke. 'My back goes out more often than I do these days.'

'That's actually almost funny,' said Ann. 'You should write that down.'

Luke took out a pen and a wallet from the inside of his coat pocket and located a piece of paper that was folded into quarters. He unfolded it, looked fondly at its content briefly, then turned it over to the blank side and began to write.

ACKNOWLEDGEMENTS

The author would like to thank Bill W, Bruce Lloyd, Charlotte Atyeo, Steve Leard, Alex Arlett, Jack Ridley, Oli Munson, Amanda Smith, Matt Williams, Jane Purdon and Amanda Newbery.

BY THE SAME AUTHOR

(Writing as Ian Ridley)

FICTION

Outer Circle

(Book 1, Jan Mason: Investigative journalist series)

Don't Talk

(Book 2, Jan Mason: Investigative journalist series)

NON-FICTION

The Breath of Sadness

On love, grief and cricket